popularity
contest

Look for more books in

The Friendship Ring Series:

Rachel Vail's

The Friendship Ring Series

popularity
contest

AN APPLE PAPERBACK / SCHOLASTIC INC.

New York • Toronto • London • Auckland • Sydney
Mexico City • New Delhi • Hong Kong

ISBN 0-590-68911-8

Copyright © 2000 by Rachel Vail.
All rights reserved. Published by Scholastic Inc.

SCHOLASTIC, APPLE PAPERBACKS, and associated logos
are trademarks and/or registered trademarks of Scholastic Inc.

12 11 10 9 8 7 6 5 4 3 2 1   0 1 2 3 4 5/0

Printed in the U.S.A.   40
First Scholastic printing, February 2000

one

"I nominate Zoe Grandon," Morgan Miller said, and then quickly sat down in the seat beside me again, dropping her head forward so her dark hair swung in front of her face.

"Thanks," I whispered.

On the other side of me, tiny Olivia Pogostin was standing, her thin arm raised above her pigtailed head. When she was called on, she said, "I second the nomination." Her face was serious and solemn, like this was the U.S. Senate or something instead of just the sticky-floored same old Boggs Middle School auditorium.

"Thank you, Olivia," said Mrs. Johnson, the principal.

I smiled at Olivia, then turned the other way and smiled at Morgan. I love sitting sandwiched between two friends, especially in an assembly instead of in band, since practicing clarinet is a little low on my list of priorities. It was turning into a good day. I'd had Mallomars in my lunch, and then, afterward, we played basketball. It was 20–17, us, when Morgan drilled me the ball, which jammed my ring finger, but I kept my hands on it and put it up for a perfect layup for the win just as the bell rang. We all jumped around like a bunch of lunatics, screaming. And now getting nominated, and sitting between my friends.

I rubbed my ring finger. It was still a little swollen, but it didn't really hurt. I wiggled the knot part of my new friendship ring around my finger. Still loose enough, so my finger wasn't broken or anything. Just bruised. I looked at my ring. It really is pretty, perfect for me and my best friend, CJ Hurley — strong, simple, pretty. The ring, I mean.

I glanced at Morgan while I rubbed my ring. She had the identical ring on, which didn't bother me, so much, anymore. I have always been friends with Morgan and everybody else in the grade, so just because I now have a BEST friend doesn't mean I have to be a nervous wreck that CJ is about to dump me and go back to being best friends with Morgan. That's ridiculous.

I've been trying to convince myself of that. Mostly it's working. CJ chose me. And I like Morgan, and look, she obviously still likes me or she wouldn't have picked me for her team at lunch or nominated me for president of seventh grade just now. I guess it turned out good, really, that CJ invited Morgan and Olivia to get the same rings as us. CJ is more generous than I am. I'm trying to improve. I forced myself to look at the rings on Morgan's and Olivia's fingers and realized I no longer wanted to pull those rings off Morgan and Olivia the hard way, over their hands and arms and necks and heads, the way I had the day they got them.

My new level of maturity had me feeling nearly saintly in my personality, almost deserving of the fact that my friends had just nominated me and seconded me for president of the class. *Things are going well,* I thought. *Almost back to sanity.*

I unclenched my fists and smiled to myself, thinking about that beautiful layup that won the game at lunch. Mrs. Johnson asked for the second time for another nomination. "It's a democracy," she said. "We need an opponent."

That felt pretty good, that maybe a lot of people thought I'd done a good enough job last year that they wanted me to be president again. As I looked around, I noticed Tommy Levit looking back at me across the auditorium aisle and I smiled at him.

What a look he gave me, his dark eyes narrowed, like looking at me with his whole eyes was too sickening. Youch. In case I for one minute was in danger of getting a swelled head. I scrunched down on the auditorium seat, and the stiff imitation velvet scraped the backs of my thighs. Just what I needed. I wore shorts today in hopes of sweating a little less than my usual buckets, and so, in sliding down trying to disappear from the face of the earth or at least the sight of Tommy Levit, probably developed red blotches on the backs of my thighs. As if my thighs were so gorgeous to begin with that I could afford a little less blinding beauty.

Tommy is my buddy, he's been my buddy forever, and what can I do? I smile a lot, at everybody, especially if they smile at me first, and I'm not used to being hated, so I don't know how to act, during it. That's why I smiled at him.

Well, that and also because I am madly in love with the boy.

Tommy raised his hand. I smiled at him again, or tried to.

"Tommy Levit?" The principal called on him. What did he want to do? Tell on me? How? *Zoe was just gloating; she smiled at me.*

"I nominate Lou Hochstetter," Tommy said, lowering his arm.

I managed to stay on my seat, though the floor of the auditorium is so slimy, my sneaker slipped out from under me and I had to grab on to the armrests on either side of me, knocking Morgan's arm off one and Olivia's off the other. I was hyperventilating too much to apologize to either. Anyway, I decided, it was probably more important to concentrate on not falling on the floor completely.

I didn't know where Lou was sitting; somewhere right behind me, probably, but there was no way I was about to risk losing my balance on the seat again by turning around to look. I actually like Lou, a lot. More than Tommy does, in fact, or so I thought. It wasn't that I was going to have to run against him — there was inevitably going to be someone running against me for president, and since I'm friends with pretty much everybody in the grade, it was going to be somebody I like. It's just who nominated him, and how, that had me practically lurching off my chair.

Last year, Tommy was MY campaign manager. It was a great campaign, lots of fun. Tommy and his twin brother, Jonas, made most of my posters for me, all those afternoons in their tree house right on the edge of my yard and theirs.

I never should've smiled at him. That was my mistake. My latest mistake.

My body shivered without warning, and Olivia stiffened in the seat next to me. I smiled at her to show her I was OK, not losing total control of my body. Olivia is petite and restrained, which just made me feel that much more like a hyperactive hippopotamus.

Somebody toward the back of the auditorium seconded the nomination, and the principal, Mrs. Johnson, asked if there were any more nominations for president of the seventh grade. There weren't, so she moved on to eighth. Me against Lou, and that was all.

Morgan leaned close to my head and whispered into my ear, "Don't worry, Zoe. You'll definitely beat Lou."

I tried to smile at her, but the effort made me feel like crying, so I gave it up and closed my eyes.

"You're the incumbent," Olivia whispered to me, and since I had no idea what that means, I gave her a silent chuckle and half-nod — the kind where you just lift your chin a little and raise your eyebrows. When my sister Colette does that, she looks very knowing.

Morgan asked me what Olivia just said.

I turned to Morgan and whispered through her shiny hair, "I have no idea. I think she called me a cucumber."

"A what?"

"She said, 'You're the cucumber.'"

Morgan slapped her hand over her mouth and opened her dark eyes wide.

I got the giggles, and my hand didn't hold them in well enough. From up on the auditorium stage, Mrs. Johnson gave me a disappointed look. I took a deep breath, but out of the corner of my eye, I could see Morgan's shoulders shaking next to me and had to lower my head into my lap.

When I was close to stopping, Olivia asked, "What are you laughing at?"

I slid down onto the grimy floor with both hands over my mouth. Morgan crouched beside me, whispering "You're the cucumber?"

"Mmm-hmm. You think it's a compliment?" Tears were running down my face, but what Morgan didn't know was they weren't just from laughter.

The eighth-grade nominations flashed by while we were down there on the floor; I couldn't even listen and I'm normally very nosy. I double-bowed my new red shoelaces, trying to get my hands to stop shaking. Morgan sighed a few times. When we were calm, we hoisted ourselves back up onto the seats. Olivia whispered to me, "Are you making fun of Lou?"

"No!" I whispered back.

Olivia stared straight forward. She's very moral. The rest of us disappoint her pretty often.

"Olivia," I whispered again. "I was making fun of myself. Seriously. About how stupid I am."

Olivia whispered, "Shh." Mrs. Johnson was reminding us how important class elections are, that they're not supposed to be just popularity contests, blah, blah, blah. What we hear every year. No way Olivia, even, could be all that interested.

"Did you call me a cucumber?" I tried asking her.

"Shh," she said again, more insistently. I tried forcing myself to concentrate on the boring announcements but I failed. When Mrs. Johnson finally dismissed the seventh grade and the flipping noise of all the chairs slapping up into their folded positions startled me out of my daydreaming, I couldn't stop myself. I had to look over at Tommy. He was staring at me, and not in a friendly way. Every time he looks at me now, it's like that — head lowered and mouth tight, glaring out from under his dark, straight eyebrows.

He used to smile every time he saw me.

two

After the assembly, Morgan, Olivia, and I walked past the principal's office, where my best friend (I love saying that), CJ Hurley, was sitting. She has in-school suspension for forging her mother's name on her permission slip to go apple picking yesterday, so she'll be on that chair for the rest of the week. Morgan, Olivia, and I gave her sad faces and secret waves, down near our hips, as we passed her. CJ was sitting straight in her chair, at attention as always, her pale green eyes wide and round, and her frizzy light brown hair in a ponytail instead of a bun, since she quit ballet.

That ponytail made me feel really sad. CJ is an incredibly talented ballerina even if she thinks she's not good enough. I'm definitely psyched she'll be playing soccer this year instead of always rushing off to ballet. I just think she shouldn't have quit something she loves so much. But she stopped being best friends with Morgan because Morgan was always telling her what to do, and her mother, too, so I make sure I just listen and sometimes say *well, that's true* when something is. I never had a best friend before her, so I'm not sure if that's what you're supposed to do, but that's what I usually do with plain friends.

Morgan and Olivia gave their little waves and sad faces and kept going. Everybody knows you're not allowed to talk to someone in in-school suspension or you get detention and can't go to soccer. I slowed down, though, and then stopped in front of her, feeling too sad about her ponytail-instead-of-a-bun.

CJ tilted her head, like, *get out of here*, but I just stayed, wishing there were something I could say to cheer her and myself up. CJ is never a very smiley person anyway, but she looked like a hostage the way she was sitting there, so determined and still, clutching the sides of her chair.

Morgan turned around, saw me, ran back, and yanked me away by the arm. When I looked over my shoulder at CJ, she was staring forward again.

"Poor CJ," I said as we got to our lockers.

Morgan and Olivia both shook their heads. "Can you believe she forged her permission slip?" Morgan asked. I was there when she forged it, so of course I believed it. "It seems so un-CJ," Morgan added, yanking her lock open.

I didn't say anything, as tempted as I was to explain and show off how close I am with CJ. I resisted telling them that CJ's mother never would've let her go on the apple-picking trip, since CJ was supposed to be in ballet class yesterday afternoon, and how important it was to CJ to feel like a normal seventh grader by going on the class trip. It had made sense to me at the time, though when we got back, seeing her parents' terrified, angry faces, I felt pretty guilty. "It was a fun trip, though, huh?" I said.

"Sour," said Morgan, and I laughed because we had spent the day before spitting out apples and saying *sour*!

"CJ is usually honest," said Olivia, shaking her solemn head.

I sighed. I'd rather joke about apples.

"My mother called CJ's last night," Olivia went on. "She was a wreck." Olivia's mother and CJ's are best friends, and Morgan was CJ's best friend from fourth grade until last week. CJ isn't very competitive, but the rest of us have this thing of proving who has the most inside information about her.

"Unbelievable," Morgan whispered.

We all shook our heads. I wondered which person we were all pitying, but I didn't want to be an idiot and ask. Last year I was socially confident, but this year, for some reason, every other thing I say turns out to be the absolute wrong thing, which makes somebody furious at me or think I'm coarse.

As we were lying in the dark of our room last night, I asked my sister Devin what to do if you find yourself saying the wrong thing every time you open your mouth. She said, *Keep your mouth shut.* Devin is very cool, so I'm trying it. I lined my books up in the bottom of my locker to keep from saying anything. I wanted to get back to how much fun we'd had at apple picking yesterday.

"So it's you against Lou Hochstetter, huh?" Morgan asked me. I was about to say *I guess so* when I noticed Morgan grinning at Olivia.

"Don't," I heard Olivia whisper.

"What?" I asked. I hate being on the outside. They both shook their heads. I got so nervous I sat right down on the floor. Maybe they thought I had no chance against Lou? I've won the past two years, and Lou knows a lot about World War II artillery, but I can't see how that has much to do with being president of seventh grade. Morgan fiddled with the lock on her locker and smirked. "Come on," I begged. Olivia closed her eyes. I had this huge surge of panic. *Why are my friends suddenly turning against me?* "You guys," I pleaded, smiling at them desperately. What a loser I suddenly felt like.

"Can we just go?" Olivia asked, and started walking.

"You're the cucumber," I answered. Maybe they didn't hear me. I got myself off the floor, swung my soccer bag over my shoulder, and hurried down the hall to keep up with them. I almost made a joke about how sweaty I was, just to say something and get to normal, but then decided against it and said a silent prayer of thanks to Devin because just as I clamped my mouth shut, Tommy and Jonas Levit rounded the corner.

"Hi," Jonas said, mostly to Morgan, and blushing a little.

Morgan didn't answer. I did. I said, "Hey."

Jonas smiled at me, but then said to Morgan, "Don't you hate wasting an assembly on a Tuesday? But at least we got out of chorus yesterday."

Morgan lowered her head but said, "Seriously." The two of them sped up, making fun of the chorus teacher's enthusiasm. They both say they hate chorus, but they sure love talking about it. The rest of us take band.

"Band is so . . . " I started, but then remembered Devin's advice and forgot what I was thinking of commenting on, about band. Olivia and Tommy stared at me, waiting for me to finish. I tucked my hair behind my ear, instead.

"So — what?" Tommy asked. He sounded totally irritated.

"Are you mad at me?" I blurted out. Tommy stopped walking. After a step, I stopped, too, and looked back at him, and so did Olivia. *Can't you ever just SHUT UP?* I asked myself.

"Mad at you?" Tommy asked, squinting one eye.

Morgan and Jonas were walking back toward us. "Come on," Jonas said to Tommy. "We'll be late."

"No." He hadn't turned away from me. "Why would I be mad at you?"

It felt like a dare. We stared at each other. *The note,* I thought, but how humiliating and awful, if I ever mentioned it. I felt my right shoulder move up an inch. Tommy closed his eyes slowly, then glared up at me again, before letting himself get dragged off by his brother into the boys' locker room.

"Somebody shoot me," I said when the door had closed behind them.

"Why is he mad at you?" Olivia asked me.

"He's probably just mad because of CJ," Morgan

said. "Maybe he thinks you made her break up with him."

I tried to sound casual as I asked, "Are they broken up, then, you think?" As if I didn't care one way or the other.

"She said she didn't like him yesterday morning, practically to his face," Morgan pointed out.

"It wasn't official," Olivia said. "But he did hear her, that was clear."

"Who cares, anyway?" Morgan turned to me and jammed her fists into her hips. "Do you really care?" She looked ready to fight.

"No," I quickly lied. "Why should I care?" I smiled as best I could.

Morgan stared at me for another second then slid her eyes away. I breathed. Morgan turned and stalked into the locker room. I made a face at Olivia like *youch*, but she didn't smile at it, so I just smiled like *just kidding* and held the heavy locker-room door open for her.

As we were strapping on our shin guards, Olivia said, "So maybe that's why Tommy's mad at you."

"Why?" I asked, trying to sound casual instead of nervous.

"Maybe he really likes CJ and thinks you turned her against him."

I tried not to die. I closed my eyes and didn't say, *That is not why at all! He has a very good reason for being mad at me, and it is the opposite of he really, really likes CJ.* Instead I managed to croak, "He did seem mad, didn't he?"

Olivia nodded very sincerely.

"I can't handle anybody being mad at me," I whispered.

"I thought you and he were good friends," Olivia said, tying a double knot.

"Yeah, well," I told her. "We used to be."

three

"**A**nything wrong?" my sister Devin asked me as she flopped down on the couch. She propped her feet on my lap, and at the same time reached into the package of Fig Newtons in my hand and helped herself to one.

"No." I flipped the page in the catalog I was searching. "I was nominated for president."

"Again?"

"Hey," our older sister, Bay, said, turning up the volume.

The three of us stared at the TV, quietly chewing our Fig Newtons, until the commercial. Then, as I went back to my catalog, Devin gave me some quick, hard rabbit kicks to the thighs and asked, "So, what's wrong? You can tell us."

"Nothing!"

"Mmm. Obviously."

Devin and I share a room, which must explain why she reads my mind. It never annoyed me really until this year, when I started having emotions beyond hungry. I slapped her on the foot and looked over her to Bay, and asked, "Hey, Bay — does Colette get all up in your business?"

"Colette?" Bay asked, without taking her eyes off the commercial.

"You know, Colette," Devin teased. "The weird one, lives in your room? Skinny, curly hair? Pierced belly button? Lots of eye shadow?"

Bay threw a pillow at Devin's head. "Oh, that Colette."

Bay never answers a question straight. I like that about her.

"So?" Devin kicked me some more. "What's wrong with you? Something to do with Tommy?"

"Shut up," I warned. Devin never lets a thing drop. It's what I don't like about her. Well, that and how pretty she is. Of the five of us, she's the only one who never goes through an awkward stage. I flipped another page in my catalog.

"So why are you acting so weird?"

"I'm not. I'm looking for something. For my campaign."

"Oh," Devin said sarcastically. "Your campaign."

Our show came back on, so we went back to watching like zombies.

The back door slammed, but I didn't really register it until Mom stormed into the TV room, shut off the TV, and dropped three pairs of cleats on the floor in front of her.

"Sorry," I said.

Mom stormed out.

Devin shrugged. Bay held the clicker out and turned our show back on. I didn't really feel like watching anymore, so I flipped through my catalog some more until I found what I was looking for. I stood up.

"Hey!" Devin complained as her feet thumped onto the floor.

I went into the kitchen. "Mom?"

"Something's wrong with the garbage disposal." She had her arm in the sink, which was half-filled with gunky brownish-gray water, up to her elbow. "If one more thing goes wrong today, I don't know . . ."

"Mom?"

Mom turned away from the sink and leaned against it, with her one arm still in it.

"Um," I said. I smiled at her. "How was work?"

She grunted. "How's your cousin holding up?"

"Fine, I guess. You know Gabriela," I said, picturing her. "She's always smiling no matter what."

"Poor Gabriela." Every time Mom mentions Gabriela's name she sighs. "Breaks my heart to think of that child wandering around with her suitcase."

"At least they let her bring her cat back and forth," I said, trying to cheer Mom up. "How is Uncle Pete holding up?"

She breathed in through her nose, which means she's either really angry or the national anthem is playing at the Olympics. "He fell asleep on the mechanic's creeper under a car again."

"Maybe he's bored," I suggested.

Mom shook her head sadly. "I never saw anybody so gifted with a wrench."

"Other than Daddy," I corrected. Uncle Pete is Mom's younger brother, so Mom has always been his protector, but my father can fix anything, even though he's a baker instead of in the car business like Mom's whole family.

"Yes, well, except when he starts doing repairs with duct tape."

"He says duct tape fixes anything," I explained. "He told me it's the best invention since Velcro."

Mom blinked a couple of times and sighed. "Your father is a good man." She jiggled her hand deep in the sink's throat and scowled.

"Why does Uncle Pete keep falling asleep?" I asked. "Is it because of their divorce?"

"None of your business, missy."

"Is something going on? Gabriela always just acts like things are fine."

"Well, how else should she act? You don't hang out your dirty laundry for the neighborhood to see." Mom pulled her wet arm out of the sink and regarded it with disappointment. "I can't fix this. Did you want something? Or just to gossip?"

"Pencils," I said.

Mom looked at me skeptically as she dried her arm on the dish towel.

"I was nominated for president and . . ."

"Again?"

"And I was thinking maybe this year instead of oak tag and all that, it would be cool to get campaign pencils — you know — ZOE GRANDON FOR PRESIDENT printed on them." I showed her the page in the catalog. Next to the photo of pencils were the words, *Pencils for everybody! For every occasion!*

Mom took the catalog from me and squinted at the picture, then lifted her reading glasses, which were dangling around her neck from a chain Colette had made her a few years ago. Anything positive Colette does gets a lot of attention.

"But you need a credit card," I explained. "And,

please, Mom? It would be so cool, don't you think? So if I could have an advance on my allowance, we could just order them. Do you think we need to do the rush delivery? It's an extra eight dollars and ninety-five cents." I crossed my fingers, hoping she was thinking about it and not just going to say, *Absolutely not — do you know what it costs to satisfy every whim of five girls?* Sometimes she's too exhausted to say yes to things.

She frowned. "When is the election?"

"Two weeks from today." I tried not to say *yippee!* Asking questions is an excellent sign.

"Plenty of time," she said, poking the catalog. 'Within five business days,' see here?"

I looked where she was pointing. "OK. So regular then. Can I? Don't you want to support my originality? Nobody ever did pencils before, I bet. What do you think, please? I will definitely pay you back, and do extra chores around the house if you want, and . . . "

"Primaries or pastels?" Mom asked, taking her glasses off.

That had to mean yes. "What do you think about the gold and silver?"

Mom nodded. "Nice, but then the name is printed in white. See?"

"Oh," I said. "You're right." She grunted approvingly of my good sense in agreeing with her. "How about . . . " I pointed at the black pencils, with names printed in gold.

Mom tilted her head to the side. Her curly reddish hair was gathered in a plastic clip in the back, her new style, which looks a little strange, like purposely messy. She nodded. "Those are sharp."

"Not yet," I said. She rolled her eyes. "I love you, Mom!"

"And I'm beautiful?"

"And you're beautiful," I repeated, psyched.

"Yeah, yeah." Mom doesn't like mushy stuff. She picked up the kitchen phone, sighing. "Just ZOE GRANDON?"

"FOR PRESIDENT. It'll fit, I counted. OK?"

She shook her head, but there was a little smile on her mouth.

"You want me to call Daddy about the garbage disposal?" I offered.

"You just get upstairs and do your homework or something, huh?"

"OK." I gave her a loud, sloppy kiss on the cheek. "Thanks, Mom."

She shooed me away. "And put those filthy cleats where they belong!"

four

In the morning, sunlight streaking in through the kitchen window makes it hard to get a clear view. I shaded my eyes with my hand. I was right. It was Tommy, tossing his book bag over the fence from his yard to mine. I dropped my hand over my eyes and leaned against the counter for balance. When I dared look again, Tommy was on top of the fence, his feet kicking out to the side as he pivoted over his left hand. He landed in my backyard and picked up his bag.

There was a wet line across my T-shirt, from where water had soaked the counter I'd been pressed against, staring out the window at Tommy. I rubbed the line of water with my hand, but you can't brush off a water spot. I looked out the window again. Tommy was leaning against the fence, licking his bottom lip, a new habit of his. I closed my eyes again. I can't watch him do that.

His family has always lived behind mine; he and his twin brother, Jonas, and I have been friends since before we all went to nursery school together. I was never weird around Tommy until seventh grade started, a few weeks ago, when I started noticing things about him like the lip licking. I can't stop seeing how dark his eyes are, and how deep his dimples indent, and the way he walks with his shoulders back. The fact that his voice has a slightly gravelly sound in it is practically killing me.

I'm whacked, obviously, totally sick, staring out the window at my backdoor neighbor with my heart pounding so hard all I could think was what if I have a heart attack and the paramedics find me dead on my kitchen floor? It'd be in the paper that I died from staring at Tommy Levit. KILLED BY A HAIRCUT, the headline would be. Short in back and longer on top, so it's shiny dark and slightly cowlicky — it really felt like his new haircut was killing me. I never noticed his hair last year and I definitely didn't used to go so psycho, just looking at it. He was always just my buddy, Tommy, with the lousy tennis serve, the quick comebacks, always up for whatever game.

I should throw an "I hate Zoe" party. That's probably the only way we'd get together, now, since we'd both go to that party for sure.

Devin sprinted past me and grabbed her lunch off the counter.

"I thought you'd left already," I couldn't help taunting.

"Yeah, well." She banged the screen door open. The high school bus comes to the bus stop earlier than the middle school bus, which I'm the only one of the five of us still taking. If you miss the bus in our family, nobody is about to drive you, either, unlike in Tommy's family. In our family, you're late? You walk. Devin walks at least once a month. I never miss the bus. OK, that's not so impressive, I know, but hey, nobody ever called me an overachiever. I'm the fifth of five girls. You take whatever unique accomplishment you can manage.

As late as she was, Devin couldn't resist pausing on the back porch to smile back at me through the screen door. "Somebody waiting for you?" she asked.

I never should've told her what happened with Tommy. I looked at my watch, hinting how late she was.

"Nice spot," she said, pointing at the bottom of my shirt. Then she smiled her little knowing smile and dashed down the walk. She thinks she's so great just because she's the prettiest of us five and never looks a mess, even in this heat. I tried rubbing the water spot, but it wasn't fading.

Tommy waved at Devin as she passed him, a little flick of his wrist. I think he might have a crush on her. Everybody does.

"Zoe just has to change," Devin yelled. "She'll be right out."

Tommy shrugged minimally. He balanced one high-top on its heel and rocked it back and forth. Waiting. It was obvious he was waiting. For me?

I picked up my lunch and books and opened the screen door. Tommy lifted his eyebrows, as if he were surprised to see me coming out my own back door.

"I didn't change," I blurted, tugging my T-shirt away from my body.

"Oh, well." He shrugged. "You win some, you lose a lot."

I felt my face heating up. I have always been able to snap right back at any insult. Nothing was coming. I hate when that happens. I thought of saying, *I was talking about my shirt, not my personality,* but then I knew he'd say something like *either way* and I'd feel even more self-conscious. I just stood there on the back porch, tugging at the bottom of my oversized red T-shirt, wishing I'd changed into anything else, maybe even the embarrassingly tight little brown top I'd worn the day he liked me.

He licked his lower lip again.

"Beat you to the bus stop," I yelled, jumping off the porch. Without looking over my shoulder to see if he was following me, I tore across the backyard and hurdled the row of low bushes my father had put in over the summer. Luckily Dad was already at work, or he'd have chased after me himself and dragged me back to the house to make me walk on the walk like a normal person. I skidded around the corner onto the sidewalk and although I was already sweating, which my friends have recently decided is a disgusting thing, I didn't slow down because I heard Tommy's footsteps behind me, gaining on me.

I'm a decent runner, but books in one arm and lunch in the other hand didn't help my cause. I pumped my legs faster, faster. *GO!* I yelled inside my head.

His elbow bumped mine as we neared the corner. I had the inside, so I boxed him out with not such a hard nudge, very fair in my opinion, and sped up. I heard myself grunt.

I got to the STOP sign first. I dropped my lunch and books, leaped up, and slapped the sign with my palm. It made a *doing!* sound.

Tommy bent over, hanging onto the bottoms of his shorts. I did the same. We were both breathing really heavy, sweat dripping off our foreheads onto our stuff that was all mixed up together in a pile between us. We stayed like that for a minute or so. I didn't want to look up at him. I thought he should say something first, since I won.

"What?" he finally asked, after I stared at him long enough.

"Beat you," I said.

He panted, "You threw an elbow."

"Did not!"

He spat on the ground. I almost spat on top, but he said something last week about how I'm like one of the guys. Since then I've been trying to be more lady-like. I don't know much about being a lady, but even I know spitting isn't up there with high heels and nail polish.

"You're just slow," I added instead.

He sorted through the pile of books, picking out his own stuff, instead of answering me.

"Ouch," I said, trying my hardest to get some response, any response. "That was a good comeback."

He looked up the street toward where the bus wasn't yet.

I kneeled down to gather up my books and said,

without looking at him, "Yeah, well, I'm gonna whomp your boy Lou in the election."

Tommy answered, "In your dreams." He wiped some sweat off his face up into his hair as the bus heaved itself groaningly around the corner. "You only won last year because I ran such an amazing campaign."

"Oh, please!" I yelled. "Who's dreaming now?"

Jonas was sprinting up the street toward us, his curly brown hair bobbling around on top of his head. He's always late, like Devin. "Hi, Jonas," I yelled above the bus's screeching breaks, so it sounded like Jonassssss.

"Hi," he said in his sweet, high voice. It hasn't started to change at all. Stepping onto the bus, he complained to Tommy, "I thought you were waiting for me."

I turned to see Tommy's reaction and caught him looking at me. I grabbed hold of the bus banister and quickly focused on my own hand, clenching it. *Nice friendship ring,* I thought, and at the same time, *So I guess he wasn't waiting for me.* Oh, well. I tugged a few times at my T-shirt to cool off my sweaty body. I smiled and said to Jonas in a jolly way, "He was embarrassing himself, trying to beat me to the bus stop."

"She beat you?" Jonas asked, slipping into a seat.

"By a mile," I said. I sat down in an empty seat across the aisle.

Tommy looked at the space next to me, then at me, and sat down next to Jonas. "I let her win," he told Jonas.

"In your dreams," I answered back.

five

The morning went by without me, sort of, like I was watching a movie of a girl like me — sitting in class, walking through the halls, going to her locker. I was kind of watching the scene at the lockers, watching myself watch Morgan pull a small plastic bag out of her backpack and shove it into her locker, and out of my mouth came, "Jacks! Is that jacks?" My loud voice startled us all.

"Yeah," Morgan said, her head bowed so her hair hung over her face.

"You like jacks?" Olivia asked her.

"No."

I shrugged at Olivia, who pushed at her bottom lip with her tongue. She just got her braces last week, and I think she's really uncomfortable. She keeps slurping and looking embarrassed about it. We keep telling her not to worry.

"My dad sent them in the mail." Morgan dumped her math and science stuff into her locker. "Jacks, he sends." She and Olivia stared at each other. I guess they're best friends now. My best friend was on the chair outside the principal's office again, so I had nobody to make meaningful eye contact with. I put my books in the bottom of my locker. Morgan and Olivia didn't look at me.

So I said cheerfully, "That was nice of your dad. Just for nothing?"

"Yeah," Morgan said with a laugh that didn't sound the slightest bit happy. "Just for 'Here, kid, knock yourself out. No money for food, but I'm such a great dad, here's some jacks!'"

"Oh," I said. Morgan was glaring at me like she might bite me. Or cry. I was hoping for bite me because making people cry I can't handle at all. I looked to Olivia for help, but her eyes were closed. I had to come up with something myself. "Well . . . " I started, without an idea what to say after that, when the bell rang. I grabbed my lunch and closed my locker. There was no lunch in Morgan's locker, only an apple from the trip Monday. *Jacks instead of lunch* was all I could think. "I love jacks," I said.

"Yeah, right." Morgan blew air from the corner of

her mouth up toward her bangs. She didn't bother to close her locker.

"I do," I insisted. "Bring 'em. Let's play after lunch."

Morgan lifted her intense eyes slowly to meet mine. I can never tell what she's thinking, maybe because her eyes are so dark you can't even see the pupils and her bangs hang in them.

"May as well," I added. "It was such a thoughtful gift. . . . " I knew that was risky thing, being sarcastic about somebody's father. But I was pretty sure I saw the edges of her lips turning up a little, so I pressed my luck. "Just think how proud he'd be if you became jacks champion of the world."

Morgan raised her long, thin arm and plucked the bag of jacks off the top shelf of her locker. "He'll take all the credit."

"And he'll deserve it," I said.

Olivia was staring at me, shaking her head as a warning to be careful and shut up, but I felt like it was OK when Morgan slammed her locker shut and said, "Oh, absolutely. After all he's given me. I mean, this thing cost almost two dollars." She pointed at the orange price sticker, pretend-impressed.

"Plus postage," I said.

"True," Morgan said, nodding. "So generous. How could I fail?"

"With a father like him," I finished for her.

She added, "Who needs enemies?"

I was getting a little nervous that we were on fragile turf here, so I resisted my impulse to keep going. Olivia's eyes were wide and tense. I smiled at Morgan.

She gave a slow blink and smiled with half her mouth, sort of a lopsided smile.

"Should we eat?" Olivia asked quietly.

"Yeah," I said enthusiastically. I don't know about Morgan but I was relieved at the suggestion, anything to get out of there without a meltdown. The three of us practically ran to the cafeteria to gobble our lunches as quickly as possible, so we could get outside to the jacks tournament.

"Just think," I said with my mouth half full because I couldn't wait to make Morgan smile again. "You'll be on the cover of *Teen People* — Morgan Miller, Cracker Jacker!"

She did smile and even took a bite of the apple in front of her. We'd be bringing apples until all the ones from our apple-picking trip Monday turned mealy. Up and down the table an apple rested on every brown lunch bag. The smell was overpowering even the mashed potato/chocolate pudding/paste smell that normally dominates the cafeteria.

Olivia was the only one without an apple, because

of her new braces. She was still on mushy food and, in fact, was eating banana baby food from a jar with a plastic spoon. She swallowed a spoonful and shyly smiled, her braces gleaming from behind her light brown lips, and said to Morgan, "Maybe you'll even get a scholarship to college."

I laughed a little more than that joke deserved, for her effort. Olivia is probably the smartest kid in our class not counting Ken Carpenter, but funny she's not. She never cracks jokes, and boy did she look nervous, trying.

Morgan answered, "Yeah, well, I'll need one."

Olivia looked down into her baby food. "Sorry."

"No," Morgan told her, touching her shoulder. "That was . . . it's OK."

"Huh," laughed Olivia awkwardly. "Hey! You know how out of it I am? I almost forgot that today is the first day of autumn!"

Neither of us knew what to say. After a minute, Morgan said, "Imagine that!" Morgan and I cracked up. Poor Olivia. She's too smart to be stuck with dopes like us. She should hang out with Ken Carpenter and maybe Roxanne Luse, who, on the other hand, is way too barreling-through-life a person, even if she's brilliant. So, no, Olivia — all fourteen pounds of her, including her pigtails — is stuck with losers who get their day made by somebody saying autumn.

"What?" Olivia asked while Morgan and I were clonking our heads on the table, laughing so hard.

Morgan draped her arm around Olivia's narrow shoulders and whispered, "Come on, let's go outside. It stinks in here." Olivia didn't even finish her baby food, she jumped up so fast, and we all went out to the playground.

In the corner of the playground where a small stone planter-border meets the chain-link fence, Morgan tore open the plastic bag. There was a full set plus four of silver jacks, two Superballs, and a red vinyl case to hold the set, after. It was actually sort of cute. My father would never think to buy me anything, especially something cute. But maybe if they were divorced, it would be different. My dad only buys things for the dog.

We flipped for first. Olivia won. I hadn't played jacks in a while so it took me a couple of turns to get going. I'm pretty good at games, usually, but my hands are beefy like my father's and better for basketball or rowing a boat than something as delicate as jacks. My father says of all of us I'm the one who should inherit his bakery because I have baker's hands, strong for pounding dough. I don't know what I want to be when I grow up so who knows, maybe I will, if he really wants me to.

I was daydreaming about that while Morgan was

having her turn, getting all the way up to sixies, when I noticed she grazed one of the cart jacks with her pinkie. "My turn," I called, and gathered up the extra jacks to get ready.

"What are you talking about?" Morgan demanded.

"The . . ." I started. "You, your pinkie moved the jack — the one that was over here." I pointed to the place on the concrete where the jack had been before she knocked it.

"I did not," Morgan growled.

"You didn't feel it?"

"I didn't touch it," she said. "So how could I feel it?"

We both looked at Olivia, but she quickly said, "I wasn't watching." Lou Hochstetter, my rival for the presidency, was loping across the playground toward us with Gideon Weld, and Olivia was watching them instead of the game.

Morgan glared at me again. "Are you saying I cheat?"

"No," I said. My behind started feeling really prickly on the concrete, so I shifted around a little. "But come on, Morgan. You definitely touched it."

"Ooh," Gideon said, his Adam's apple jumping around wildly in his long, skinny neck. "A fight."

"I did not," Morgan said.

"Fight!" Gideon yelled. "Fight!"

"We're not fighting," I told him, and smiled at Morgan, who didn't smile back. "What am I up to, fours?" I tossed the jacks out but my hands were shaking and they went pretty far apart. One of them landed on Morgan's foot.

"No, Zoe," she said. "You win. Hooray for you." She stood up, and the jack that had been on her foot skittered across the concrete of the playground.

"Come on," I said, squinting up into the sun at her.

"Who even cares?" Morgan asked. She grimaced at me as if she had a sour taste in her mouth for real. "It's just a stupid game. You win. Happy?" She blew the bangs out of her eyes impatiently and turned to Lou. "You better watch out, Lou — Zoe hates to lose so bad, you never know what she'll do in the election."

"Morgan," I said, but she wasn't looking at me so I cupped my hand over my eyes and squinted up at Lou. He shrugged. He at least knows I wouldn't do anything wrong to him. I think. "I don't . . ." I said, but I wasn't even sure what to protest, I felt so confused and sucker-punched. "I'm sorry," I finished, and my voice was shaking. I didn't trust myself to stand up; I was too off-balance. I rested one palm on the concrete to keep from tipping over, but then Morgan snapped her head toward me, and I thought, *whoops,* that was obviously the wrong thing to do, so I gathered her jacks together and tried to smile up at her, innocently. She slid her eyes away from me and yanked Gideon Weld's sleeve. He bent down, so she could whisper in his ear. He'd never been whispered to by such a pretty girl as Morgan; his Adam's apple jiggled faster than ever while he listened.

"Maybe I saw wrong," I offered, although I didn't see wrong. She had definitely touched that jack.

"Whatever," Morgan said slowly, shaking her head at me. "Come on, Olivia."

The four of them started walking back into the building. I quickly grabbed the little red vinyl bag and tried to shove the jacks in, but my hands are so meaty and clumsy, especially when I'm in a rush, and so sweaty at that point that a few of the jacks didn't make it in.

"Hey!" I called after them. "Your jacks!"

I saw Morgan bend down and whisper something in Olivia's ear. Olivia stopped in the doorway on the way back into school, cupped her hands around her mouth, and yelled back to me, "Morgan says you can keep them!"

six

"I knew you wouldn't be up here doing homework all this time," Devin said, flopping down on my bed and on the way kicking one of the jacks.

"Hey," I complained. I gathered all the jacks together and started again from the beginning, with flipping. I only managed to keep two of them in my hands. The rest plinked around our floor.

"Good one," Devin commented. I wasn't in the mood. I bounced the multicolored ball and went to work collecting one jack at a time. "Wow, you're a barrel of laughs tonight," Devin said. I threw the jacks for twosies. "Mom's cursing at the sink," Devin told me. "It's clogged again so AM and Colette got out of washing the dishes."

I concentrated on the jacks. Got them, each pair, the ball tapping out a rhythm on our wood floor. I tossed out the set for threesies, still in rhythm, and picked up the singleton first. "Cart," I said, and without pausing, tossed the ball up to try for the first set of three, near the leg of my bed. My hand collided with Devin's foot, which she'd lowered purposely to kick the jacks. "Hey!" I looked up at her. She was grinning, the jerk. "Get your fat foot off my jacks!"

"Sensitive," she said.

I replaced the jacks about where they'd been and started over, tossing the ball in the air. She caught it. "Devin!" I yelled. She can be so annoying. She hid the ball under her hip on my bed. I grunted and told her, "Next year when Anne Marie goes to college, I'm moving into her room."

"I wish," Devin said, "but Colette already has dibs. We're stuck with each other until Bay goes."

"Ugh."

"Think how I feel," Devin complained. "I can't wait to go to sleep without your snoring."

"I don't snore."

"The whole house shakes."

I never knew that. "Gross," I admitted.

"Incredibly," Devin agreed.

I picked up a few jacks and jiggled them in my

palm, thinking about that. When Devin sleeps over a friend's, I sneak into Anne Marie's room or Bay and Colette's and camp out on the floor. I don't think I've ever in my life spent a whole night in a room all alone. I doubt I'd be able to sleep.

"I really snore?" I asked her. "Loud?"

"Only when you're on your back. Don't worry."

"Oh," I said. "That's good, then, I guess. I should maybe prop myself up or something."

"Yeah," she agreed, tossing the jacks ball in the air and catching it. "Especially if you're on a sleepover. Bad enough in front of your own family. And Tommy and Jonas."

"What about them?"

"Tommy told me he's heard you snoring. It keeps him up."

"Liar," I said. I knew she was just teasing, but my cheeks were hot anyway. I held out my hand toward her, without daring to raise my eyes. "Give me that ball."

"Try to get it," Devin said.

Normally I would've jumped on top of her and wrestled her for it, but I just wasn't in the mood. It had been a pretty stressful day, and I just felt unsociable for the first time in my life. "Come on," I tried, and almost started crying. Like some baby. I sniffed it in.

"What's wrong with you?" she asked. I don't know if she really wanted to know or if she was just taunting me as usual.

"Nothing! I was just trying to play a game! OK?"

"You are so sensitive about Tommy, it's shocking." She dropped the ball on my head. It bounced off and rolled across the floor, under her bed.

"You're the one who keeps talking about Tommy," I pointed out. "I'm just trying to play jacks! I'm in the middle of a game! That's all I care about."

"If that's true, it's so sick."

"What's sick about it?"

"I never saw anybody take winning games so seriously as you," she said, getting off my bed and crushing one of the jacks under her shoe, on the way.

"I do not," I argued weakly. I didn't even convince myself.

She spun around. "Are you kidding me? You're sitting up here all alone and you're obsessed. You can't even stand to lose against yourself."

I buried my face in my hands. She had a point.

"You can't even let yourself flirt with Tommy. You have to smash him to bits just hitting tennis balls against his garage." She swept her long blond hair off her face, sighing. "You're not supposed to beat up on the boy you like."

I sighed. "Well, there goes my strategy."

"You really are pathetic," Devin said, shaking her head and laughing. "Was that really your flirting strategy? Beat him up, reject him, make him feel terrible? Because . . . you may need to regroup."

"I know it," I admitted.

"Well, that's a first step." She closed our door and leaned against it.

"Oh, great. How many more steps are there?"

"You really like him, huh?" Devin asked quietly. I shrugged, then nodded, because I do, so much, like him. "You need flirting lessons," she said.

I picked up the crushed jack and tried to straighten it out but couldn't. "Flirting lessons?" I asked, trying to sound casual. "Is there such a thing?"

"Why not?" She smiled her slow, sly smile. "Get your notebook and pay attention."

seven

It took a while and some squirming, but I finally got Tommy to look at me as we waited for the bus, so I could look slowly down and away, flick my eyes back at him, then twist my shoulders and jut one hip out to the side. It was a good thing the trick was not to look back a second time, because I was making some really unattractive faces, mocking myself. I felt like a total idiot.

But Devin had said you have to do it full out, exactly as she described, and made me practice until I could do it without falling over laughing. Different boys call Devin every night, and if you're not careful taking out the trash after dinner, you're likely to get run down by some love-struck ninth grader on a bike, circling the block for her. Over the summer, an eleventh grader nearly gave me a heart attack when he threw a pebble through our window — which was open, thank you very much — and beaned me in the head with it while I was sleeping. So it's obvious that Devin knows about flirting. Luckily the bus came a minute early because I was getting a hip cramp.

As we were getting off the bus at school, Tommy muttered something either to me or to Jonas about the math quiz, so I knew it was time for flirting method number seven. I tilted my head to the side, so my hair dropped over my face, while touching his upper arm very lightly with just fingertips (don't bruise the guy!) and, laughing quietly at the back of my throat, said, "You are SO funny." Then I quickly walked away. The walking away is apparently key to making him want you, making him feel like chasing after you. Fine, whatever. I practically sprinted into school, right past all my pals. I waited at the lockers, shaking my head about what an ignorant bumbling fool I've been. I had always thought it was important to stick around, let the other person finish his thought, look him in the eye. Devin said I may need a flirtation resource room. I have to make her bed all week and take flirting lessons for an hour every night, while everybody else is studying math and vocabulary words for the SAT's. I don't mind. It turns out I am seriously dumb at flirting, so I have to train hard.

When my friends got to the lockers we all said hi except Morgan. I knew I'd be totally miserable all day if she was giving me the silent treatment, so I said, "Hey, sorry I was so weird about the jacks yesterday."

"Forget it," she said, blowing her bangs from her eyes and dropping her textbooks in.

"So I was thinking," I tried nervously. "You're still my campaign manager, right?"

She shrugged one shoulder and said, "Of course." She looked out the corner of her eyes at Olivia, who was crouched down rearranging her books.

"Well," I said, closing my locker. "I'm clueless on strategy, so . . . " I suddenly realized that it was a stupid topic to bring up, maybe; that Morgan might think I am obsessed with winning. My palms were sweating. I wiped them on my jeans and tried to think of how to change the subject. "But . . . "

"I have some ideas," Morgan said, I think. She was mumbling into her locker so I couldn't be sure.

"Oh," I said cheerfully, encouragingly, hopefully.

"What is that supposed to mean?" Morgan asked, turning to me with her jaw jutted out. "'Oh?'" she imitated.

I blinked a few times and stuttered, "It's, I, it's supposed to mean, whatever you would most hope it would mean." I banged my head against my locker. "God, Morgan, you really scare the crap out of me sometimes. I'm standing here sweating, knowing anything I say will be the totally wrong thing. How about if I just apologize ten times now and that could cover me for the rest of the day?"

Olivia laughed. I turned and looked at her, really surprised. She doesn't laugh much. Then Morgan started laughing, too, and said, "OK. Go ahead."

"Sorry, sorry, sorry, sorry, sorry." I clasped my hands in front of my heart. "Sorrysorrysorrysorrysorry."

Morgan closed her locker. "I scare you?" she asked.

"Terrify," I said.

"You, too?" she asked Olivia as we all started walking toward the classrooms.

"I'm trying to get over it," Olivia said, and then asked me, "Did you pull a muscle in soccer? You're walking funny."

"I'm OK," I said, concentrating on doing it the way Devin had said to, pelvis-front. "This is just how I walk now," I explained.

"Oh," Olivia said.

"What's that supposed to mean?" I asked.

"Whatever you would most hope it would mean," she said, and stepped into our homeroom.

"She's funny," I said to Morgan.

"I know it," Morgan said as the bell rang. "Let's plan some election strategy at lunch, OK?"

I yelled, "OK, great!" at her back as she ran down the hall.

All through lunch, Morgan, Olivia, and I tried to come up with some witty campaign slogans. Olivia had her notebook out, but mostly Morgan and I said *um,* and Olivia didn't write that down. *Apparently um isn't so witty,* I thought.

I didn't tell them about the pencils. Things were going better, so I was just trying to keep my mouth shut as much as possible. We were busy making plans about when to go to Sundries to buy oak tag and markers. I kept saying, "Whenever."

Morgan said, "Hey — I have an idea. We could use neon colors of oak tag for the posters."

Olivia nodded solemnly. "Unique."

"Great idea," I agreed, and Morgan seemed happy. *No reason we can't do both posters AND pencils,* I told myself. *Pencils are a great idea, too.* I decided to wait for the right time to mention the pencils.

"But what should we write on the oak tag?" Olivia asked just as the bell rang. We gathered up our books.

"You want to come over to my house?" I asked them. "Maybe Saturday, after the soccer scrimmage? We could work on it then."

Olivia and Morgan looked at each other before agreeing, but that was OK with me because they both said "sure" and they each smiled at me at the lockers, so what do I care if they had to check it out with each other first?

By the time I got to English/social studies, my hips were so sore I was thinking I might have to go to the nurse. *It takes practice,* Devin had told me. *You're just used to walking like a boy.* I don't know how girls got stuck with the curvy walk when boys get to just go, but all that shoving my pelvis out front and letting my shoulders lag behind, moving with thighs first, so my hips were doing overtime, while remembering to keep my head tilted sideways, resulted in my first-ever late slip. Walking like a girl takes forever and uses muscles I never used before.

"Sorry, Mrs. Shepard," I said, plopping onto my seat. My legs were just too exhausted; I needed a break from gripping them tight. I tried to let my whole clenched body relax for a few seconds and then noticed everybody copying stuff from the board. Oh, yeah. Schoolwork. I don't know how they expect us to deal with that, on top of everything else like politics and flirting and getting along. I was feeling like — disk full.

But I took out my notebook and a pen and started

copying. Magellan. Cortez. Henry Hudson. Bleh. I hate those guys. I was happy for the distraction when a note plunked onto my desk. I unfolded it; it was from Morgan. It said, *What's with CJ today? Why's she so smiley?*

I wrote back, *Seriously,* because I hadn't noticed. When Mrs. Shepard was facing the board, Morgan turned around. I shrugged and she shrugged back. Then she leaned over the note to write back. I stared out the window, wondering when Morgan had noticed CJ being smiley, and what CJ was so smiley about since she was still suspended and if I had to sit there for four whole days, in the hallway on a chair alone with nobody to talk to and no window, even, I'd go totally insane. That got me to thinking how I was feeling nearly insane anyway, hearing about Explorers for the seventh autumn in a row and my legs aching like a sprinter's. Second day of autumn, I guess.

Autumn, what a crazy word, I was thinking, when Mrs. Shepard scratched her nails on the blackboard to make us all listen up. She's a scary woman. I tried to force myself to pay attention, but within a few seconds my attention was out the window again. It's really hard for me to sit still on beautiful sunny days. I do much better when it's drizzly out. *Good thing I don't live in California,* I was thinking, *or I'd be totally ignorant.*

While I was thinking that, the note came back onto my desk. Morgan had written, *Come up with any campaign strategies yet?*

The bell rang before I could think of something not wrong to write back. Mrs. Shepard is the kind of teacher who makes you sit still until she dismisses you, so I didn't dare gather up my books until she tipped her head. Phew. Only one more class and that was gym, so at least I could stretch out. My legs were really starting to cramp.

I took the long way to gym even though I had to go to my locker first and walk my crazy pelvis-thrusting, hip-waving way. I wanted to check out CJ.

Morgan was right. She did seem smiley. She seemed perfectly happy, sitting there alone outside the principal's office. It was too weird. I decided during gym to go back there, after, instead of just kicking around soccer balls waiting for practice, like usual, and see what was wrong with her. She's my best friend, after all.

When I got there, she was walking toward the main entrance. She smiled happily at me, which made me feel better. "Only one day to go," I told her.

"It's . . . " She shrugged and kept walking, her chin tipped slightly up.

"What?" I asked. I tried to stand straighter and walk without clonking my feet, thighs first. "It's what?"

She took a deep breath. "It's not so bad."

"Being suspended? Are you kidding?"

She leaned against the heavy door to open it. I pushed with her, and we both squinted in the bright sunlight.

"It gives me time to — to think," she explained. She held her hand over her eyebrows like a visor and peered around. I looked, too, but didn't see her mother's car. She's not allowed to start soccer practice until she's done being suspended, obviously, so even though she quit ballet to be with her friends and play soccer, she can't do either yet.

"Time to think?" As I said it, I realized it sounded like I thought thinking was a ridiculous way to spend your time. That made me laugh a little. She smiled but didn't laugh along. Laughing alone is one of life's more lonely experiences, so I stopped and asked, "Have you been thinking about dance?"

"I guess," she answered. "Some."

I nodded. I wondered if she could get back into ballet. She'd made it sound like if she missed a week of classes, it was practically a good-bye kiss to any chance at a career, but that just seems a little too drastic. It would be a lot more fun for me to have her around more, rather than racing off to ballet class practically every day and weekends, too, and all of

Christmas vacation, but the more I think about it, the more I'm hoping she'll go back to it. She's just, special, and, God knows, if there were anything special about me, I wouldn't waste my time trying to hide it. I'd take out ads in the paper, I'd do those twirly things down the hallway, if I were special. But I knew it was important to let it be her decision.

I asked her, "Do you think you could go back, if you want?"

"With Tommy, you mean?"

Well, that surprised me. "Um," I think I said. "Tommy?"

"Do you think I should like him again?"

"No."

"Really?" she asked sweetly. I was gripping the bottoms of my gym shorts to keep from shaking her or tearing all my own hair out.

"Definitely not," I managed to say.

Her mother beeped. CJ held up one finger, her long, thin arm elegantly outstretched toward the circle. *I could crack that arm over my knee like a twig,* I caught myself thinking. I pushed my pelvis forward and tilted my head so my hair fell across my face. It was annoying, but part of the method. *It hurts to be beautiful,* Devin had explained.

"Oh," I said, smiling at CJ. "We were talking about

the election at lunch, and Morgan and Olivia are coming over Saturday after the soccer scrimmage. Can you come?"

"Sure," she whispered.

"Great." I put my arm around her bony shoulders. She feels a little like a skeleton. I smiled at her and whispered, "I have this idea."

"I was just," CJ whispered. "I mean, I know he, you guys are like in a, I mean you are my best friend, so I don't want to, you know, but, because this week he's been so, I don't know."

"Tommy?" Sometimes it's hard to follow anything CJ says. Sometimes she makes more sense to me than anybody in the world, even maybe including my sisters, but sometimes? Not a clue.

"Sorry," CJ said. "What did you, were you, saying? The election?"

"No, no," I protested. "What did you mean, this week he's been so . . ."

CJ smiled that little private smile again. "He just, he comes by, between every period, and sort of, you know his eyebrows?"

"Yeah?" Do I know his eyebrows. I *memorize* his eyebrows.

"He, like, raises them at me."

"Every period? Even between seventh and eighth?"

She nodded. "Isn't that cute?"

"Adorable," I admitted.

Her mother beeped again.

"So I just," she said, walking toward her mother. "But if you don't want me to . . . "

I waved good-bye and after they drove off I trudged back to the gym, not caring how much noise my feet made on the way or where my pelvis was in relation to the rest of me.

eight

CJ wasn't lying. I visited her every between-classes the next day and ended up practically joined at the hip with Tommy. I couldn't believe him; he was taking the long way, every single break, to walk by her.

We didn't talk, barely even acknowledged each other's presence. On the way from my locker after lunch before English, I dropped the pelvis-front walk in my hurry to try to get to CJ before him. I could hear his footsteps gaining on me. I waved to CJ and let him pass me, rushing to band. I don't know if he waved at her or what, but I did notice that CJ looked slowly down and away, then flicked her eyes back at him. *Does everybody know this stuff but me?*

The bell rang, making me late for band. I sped up; I don't have any musical ability and I never practice, so Mr. Ritacco, the band teacher, hates me. I tried to slip into my chair inconspicuously, assembling my clarinet on the way. No such luck. "Zoe," I heard Mr. Ritacco bellow. "Give me a *B flat* scale."

"No problem!" I said, cheerfully standing up, thinking, *No idea, absolutely no clue where to put my fingers.* I prayed and tried, but the clarinet squawked horribly. "Oops," I said. "Hold on, hold on, here we go." I blew a few notes, random notes not in any scale known to music. "Oh, oh, I got it."

Honk, went my weirdly atonal clarinet. A few people giggled. I smiled at them. My cousin Gabriela gave me her biggest, most encouraging grin. I took a deep breath.

"A minor," suggested Mr. Ritacco.

In case I thought I had ever had a sweat attack before. He wasn't letting me off the hook, and I was drenched. I was standing there alone in front of the whole band class, shaking so much I banged the clarinet's mouthpiece into my teeth. "Ouch," I said, tasting blood. "I think I just gave myself a fat lip."

"C major," said Mr. Ritacco without cracking a smile.

He didn't let me sit down until I had failed six scales

in a row, bleating like a wounded sheep and people not even laughing anymore.

Well, Tommy was.

Without really meaning to, I dared to look over at Tommy as I was melting damply into my chair. He plays first alto sax, and I play, like, last clarinet, whatever that's called, loser clarinet, so we're pretty near each other. He practices. I've heard him out in his yard. He doesn't like anybody to hear him is why he practices out there, but my window looks over his backyard, so I've seen him. Saxophone is not an easy instrument to play quietly, so I've heard him doing his scales, and with him, it's not just random notes wherever his fingers choose to cover and hope for the best, like me.

This time I wasn't feeling so hot about myself, so I didn't smile at him gloatingly. I didn't even remember to tilt my head properly. I just looked in his eyes, by habit, by accident. As soon as I realized we were making eye contact, I almost jerked my head away. I'm strong, but there's only so much a person can take. There are limits. But he smiled at me, just a little, and gently.

I smiled back, not meaning to, but it's like my face doesn't know how to stop itself when someone smiles at it. Like a mirror, it has no choice. And also I guess beyond that, what a relief! He was smiling at me like he liked me again. I knew inside that he didn't, but I let myself pretend for a few seconds.

Mr. Ritacco tapped his skinny little baton on the peeling black metal stand in front of him. Tommy tipped the mouthpiece of his saxophone up into his mouth, between his lips, but he was still smiling, so he couldn't play the first notes. I was having the same problem. *I should switch to drums,* I thought. What good is an instrument you can't play while you're smiling?

All through a very awful Boggs Middle School Band version of "When the Saints Go Marching In," I just moved my fingers randomly on the keys without blowing and tried to figure what had I done that made Tommy stop hating me.

I didn't get it until the end of class when I was pulling my clarinet apart and some spit flew out of the mouthpiece and hit me in the eye, and I heard Tommy laugh. I had failed.

I felt like I'd cracked the code. I snapped my clarinet case shut and strutted out of the band room pelvis first, happier than I'd been in a long time. If all I have to do is fail, no problem. I can fail. Anybody in band could tell you that.

Anyway, failing is way easier than succeeding, right? Or winning. You don't even have to try. In fact, you have to NOT try.

And that's how I figured out a much better election

campaign strategy than neon oak tag or pencils with ZOE GRANDON FOR PRESIDENT on them.

Because if what I really want is just for everybody to like me and not be mad at me, what I have to do is lose. What do I care about the seventh-grade election anyway? President? So what? The thing is, when Mrs. Johnson said that thing about *this should not be a popularity contest*? That is exactly what I have always thought school elections were — popularity contests. So I always sort of in my heart thought that if I won, that meant people liked me. Best.

But as I bopped down the hall with my clarinet case bumping off my legs, I realized that Mrs. Johnson was telling the truth — this election isn't a popularity contest, it's the opposite. And I'd rather win a popularity contest than an election any day.

nine

I couldn't get to sleep Friday night, from the excitement of having figured out how to make things better. Things have just been off, weird, a little awkward lately, and the fact of finally noticing what it takes to be liked in seventh grade was, like, I could breathe again. It's been so awful for me, to mess up so often and have people walking around scowling at me. I sort of didn't want to admit it, but I've been really tense in school lately, not feeling like normal-happy-everything's-OK me. And all this time it's been because I'm trying for the wrong thing. All this time I've been thinking *try harder, do better* and I end up just driving people away, so I try harder again, and my friends were really starting to hate me. I don't know why I'm so thick it took me until practically October to figure this out. *Just lose,* I wrote on an index card at 3:27 A.M. I fell asleep reading it over and over, like a magic spell or something.

I woke up Saturday psyched to try it out. It was our first intrasquad soccer scrimmage, so it was the perfect thing. "Just lose," I was whispering to myself as I tied my cleats' laces so I could swing them over my shoulder for the bike ride to the field.

"What did you say?" Bay asked, skimming down the steps past me.

"Just, um, loose," I explained. "Last time I tied my cleats in such a tight knot, I almost had to wear them tied together!"

Bay looked at me like I was a wacko and headed out the back door for her jog. She's such a great athlete. I sometimes imagine what it would feel like to beat her in anything — one-on-one basketball, a sprint — but, oops, no. Forgot. *Just lose.* I decided not to think about it too much because it hurts my brain and I could get all messed up, thinking about if that makes complete sense and what Bay would say if I talked over this new theory with her. *Concentrate,* I told myself.

Since CJ was finally free from the suspension chair, she could play. I waved as she marched flat-footed in her shiny new cleats out toward the field, her hair yanked back in its poof of a ponytail and her mother watching from the station wagon with the window rolled down. I waited on the track for her, to start the warm-up lap. As we started, I noticed she glanced quickly over to her mom. Her mother has a thing about her running, because she could twist an ankle and miss part of the ballet season. But now she'd quit, so there was no reason she couldn't run, other than the fact that her body didn't know quite how. CJ gritted her teeth and puffed along beside me, doing her weird high-knee version of running. I slowed down; bright red blotches were spreading on her cheeks.

"You OK?"

"My . . . ankles . . . hurt," she got out between huffs.

"It's the cleats," I explained. "You'll get used to it."

She nodded her head. "Do your, does it, nothing."

"What?"

"I don't mean to, does it hurt your, you know . . ."

"My what?" I asked.

CJ closed her eyes and quickly said, "Your, you know, bust."

"No. Why? Do yours hurt?"

"No," CJ answered, breathing hard. "But mine don't bounce."

I looked down at my chest. Ba-boom, ba-boom. They suddenly looked huge to me, and gross. And heaving. I crossed my arms over them to try to control their wild caroming and forced myself to smile at my flat, perfect best friend. "Now that you mention it," I said. Coach Cress blew her whistle. We jogged our slow jog over to her (me going ba-boom, ba-boom, and CJ with her knees up high in front) where we were split into teams.

CJ was on my squad — blue vests — and so was Olivia. Morgan was on the yellow vests. She made a very sad face and hugged each of us, like she was going off to a foreign land or something. *It's just a game,* I thought of saying, but kept my trap shut. I had my own plan for the scrimmage and I wasn't taking any chances right when I finally figured out how to play. *Just lose!*

So I made a sad face, too. Coach Cress blew her whistle and told us to hustle. Roxanne did a little hustle dance, which cracked me up, and we got into positions. I walked — to minimize bounce.

Morgan and I were both playing forward center, so we shot it out for first possession. I won. I hadn't meant to win, but what are you going to do? You have to put out one finger or two, and I was odds because she chose evens, and I thought she would put out one finger, so I put out one finger so she'd win, but she didn't. She put out two. It was taking all my concentration to remember what to root for; it's so complicated for my weak little brain to bend itself around *you win by losing*. At first, I said half of "Yeah!" because I was odds and there were three fingers — but like one microsecond into it, after the "Y" but before the "ah!" I realized, whoops, I was trying to lose, so I changed it to "aw." I ended up sounding like a donkey: "Yee-aw!"

Morgan gave me a confused look.

I tried to say sorry, but I was cracking up at myself for having said *yee-aw*. Coach Cress blew her whistle. I tapped the ball to Roxanne on my wing and sprinted down the field, calling myself donkey names all the way.

It took a while, but the ball came to me after a few minutes of play and trying to dodge Gabriela, my nice but boring cousin, who was supposed to be guarding me. As sweet as she is, she's not too fast on her feet. I broke away and got open, and Roxanne found me, passed the ball perfectly to my outside foot. I had a shot on goal, but it went wide. I started to swear, but then reminded myself, *No — that's good!* I shook my head and got back in position.

Gabriela was trying to keep up with me. "I've been meaning to ask you — can I help with your campaign?"

"Um," I said. Although CJ, Morgan, and Olivia were

coming over after the scrimmage to work on campaign strategy, I really wasn't intending to do any campaigning at all. In fact, since my new plan was to lose, I figured I didn't have to make a single poster. So I didn't know what to say.

"I could make posters," Gabriela offered. "I'm good at art, if you want some special drawings on them. Or whatever. I'd like to help."

"Great, sure, thanks," I said without looking away from the ball. We were back at midfield, watching her team dribble close to our goal.

"Are you mad at me?" she asked.

"Huh?" It sounded like such a wimpy, annoying question, I wanted to shoot myself, remembering having asked it myself. "Why would I be mad at you?" I heard myself ask.

"About, you know, what's going on between my dad and your mom?"

"I don't even know about it," I told her, which was pretty much true. And also we were supposed to be playing soccer. I hate when people chat through a game, I can't help it.

"Oh," Gabriela said. "I don't, either. I just heard him on the phone with her, and then, you don't want me to help with your campaign, so I thought . . . "

I wanted to reassure her that my mother isn't angry

at her father. She just has a car dealership to run, and he keeps falling asleep on the job. But as Mom said, *It's not my business.* I ran away from Gabriela toward the sideline and jumped around, waving my hand to show I was open. Roxanne kicked me a rocket. I started dribbling downfield. Gabriela was sprinting toward me. I played with the ball a little, planning to dribble around her and get the open shot on goal. But then I thought, *Oops, no.* And then, *Man, this is even harder than walking like a girl.*

I kicked the ball to Gabriela instead of trying to get the goal. A light kick, just a gentle tap, almost a dribble to my other foot but right beyond it, instead, to Gabriela's foot. Right to the girl guarding me. It was hard to get my body to do it. My stomach turned upside down as the ball clunked against Gabriela's cleat. She looked up at me, surprised. I tried not to have any expression on my face.

"Oh," she gasped, then turned upfield and walloped the ball with a thudding kick.

I lifted my hands to my face like I was disappointed in myself, but then I wasn't sure if that was right, either, so I dropped them.

"Why did you kick the ball to me?" Gabriela asked as we jogged slowly up the field.

"I didn't," I lied. "Why would I do that? You're on

the other team." I couldn't look at her. I was pissed at myself for caring, but I couldn't help it. I wanted to puke.

"Yes, you did," Gabriela insisted. "You kicked it right to me. On purpose."

I crossed my arms over my jiggly chest and told her, "It's just a game."

ten

After the scrimmage, CJ, Morgan, and Olivia all came back to my house to plan the election strategy. I reminded myself to just shut up.

"My idea is, let's think of something that rhymes with Grandon," Olivia suggested. "For the posters."

"Brandon," CJ blurted out.

"Oh, that's a good one," barked Morgan. "We could write 'Vote for Grandon! She's not Brandon!'"

"Whoever that is," I added, since we don't know anybody named Brandon.

CJ was blushing. I felt bad. So I said, "But that does rhyme. Good thing my sister Bay wasn't a boy — maybe she would've been named Brandon Grandon."

"I think your parents would've noticed," Morgan said.

We all laughed. CJ looked at me gratefully.

"I lost the scrimmage for us," I said. *An intrasquad scrimmage,* I kept reminding myself, *totally meaningless, and I did it on purpose.* But my stomach was all acidy as my mind endlessly replayed that kick to Gabriela.

"Don't worry about it," CJ said in her slow, caring way.

"Oh, I'm not worried," I assured her, all of them, quickly. "I mean, who cares, right?" I pasted a big smile on my face. None of them responded, so I kept going. "I don't. Just a scrimmage. I don't care. Even if it's a game. Or not a game, an anything. No! I was just saying I'm the one who lost it, for us. Sorry. If you care. Which you don't. Of course. Especially Morgan."

Morgan glared at me.

"No," I said quickly. "I mean, because, your team won anyway! Is all." They were all looking at me blankly, so I kept going. "Why would you? Care. I wouldn't care, if I were you, or even if I were myself. Which I am. Turns out." Olivia stuck her pencil in her mouth and chewed on it thoughtfully. "Hey," I said desperately. "That reminds me, speaking of me, I was thinking of, instead of, like, oak tag or the usual stuff, maybe ZOE GRANDON FOR PRESIDENT pencils."

The three of them looked at one another but not at me. Then Morgan laughed. "You got us," she said. "We thought you were serious for a second!"

"Ha, ha, ha," I said. "Obviously. Joking. Ha, ha, ha."

"Oh, that was a good one," Olivia said flatly, biting the pencil.

"Hey!" I said again, louder than I meant to. "Are your teeth feeling better? With the braces, I mean. You're biting."

Olivia took the pencil out of her mouth and looked at it, like it had surprised her. "Yeah," she said. "I guess I am."

"You want something to eat?" I offered, jumping up off the floor. I'm so happy to give little scrawny people food. And even happier to change the subject. My legs were shaking, and I couldn't stop moving. I grabbed a blank piece of paper and crumpled it for no apparent reason and asked, "You hungry or not?"

"Yeah!" Olivia grinned, so all her new braces showed. "I'm starving!"

"Good. This is boring, isn't it? I mean, who really cares about the election?" I slipped on the stairs; I was in such a hurry to get out of there.

In the kitchen, I took out bread and cold cuts to make us some sandwiches. "Now this is more interesting," I said enthusiastically.

"For a snack?" CJ asked.

My hands were full of plastic bags of meat, the loaf of bread, and two jars of mustard (honey mustard and country Dijon, because I didn't know which they wanted). I stopped. The refrigerator door slammed me in the behind. I almost dropped everything. "Um," I said. "I just thought, after soccer . . . If you want something else . . . " I held the refrigerator open, and the three of them peered inside. "Whatever you want, take. Really."

"I'd actually love a sandwich," Olivia said.

"Me, too," said Morgan.

"Oh," said CJ. "So would I. I was just saying."

"OK." I brought the stuff to the counter and laid out the bread.

CJ jumped up and sat on the counter, beside me. I smiled at her, happy she felt comfortable enough in my house to do that. "Cheese?" I asked her.

"Just a slice of turkey would be great," she said slowly. She pulled her friendship ring off and tried it on each of her other fingers. "Is this, do we count this as dinner? Because I ate lunch before soccer."

"This is a snack." Morgan's voice sounded really irritated. "Do you have to, like, fill out a chart for your mother or something?" She clenched her eyebrows.

"No," CJ whispered, turning her ring around and wrapping the knot part inside her tight fist.

eleven

The plan was for them to stay until four, four-thirty. At exactly four o'clock, the doorbell rang. It was CJ's mother, there to pick up CJ and Olivia both, since their families were getting together for dinner at a restaurant. CJ looked at me sadly. Even though Olivia has friendship rings with us, and even though CJ was the one who suggested Olivia and Morgan get them to match ours and make us a real clique, I still think CJ doesn't like Olivia that much. It's probably just that their two families spend so much time together, CJ doesn't feel like being friends with Olivia is her choice. And CJ has some issues with her mother about who gets to make the choices in CJ's life. I don't really have issues with my mother over anything, other than my cleats not being put away. Then again, my mother never said I was her best friend, which CJ's mother says a lot. I never thought of my mother even having a best friend, never mind it being me. She seems too busy, or too grown-up maybe, or maybe like she doesn't really need one. Maybe I just never thought about it, like I never thought about a lot of things. Things just are what they are. It occurred to me, as Olivia and CJ were putting on their shoes, that I may have missed a lot of what's been going on, my whole life. I hate that.

CJ's mother, Mrs. Hurley, was waiting in the front hall. "You must be Bay," I heard her say to Anne Marie, who was studying in the dining room.

"Anne Marie," said Anne Marie.

"Oh," said Mrs. Hurley. "Of course."

It was weird to me that anybody could confuse studious, serious Anne Marie with Bay the superjock. I listened but I guess Mrs. Hurley and Anne Marie were done talking.

"'Bye," CJ whispered to me.

"Thank you," said Olivia.

Morgan and I walked them to the door. "How's the election planning going?" Mrs. Hurley asked.

"Wow," I blurted. "I don't know if my mom even remembers I'm running."

"Mom," CJ groaned.

"What?" Mrs. Hurley shrugged.

"No," I said. "Thanks. It's . . . we're working on it."

"Great," Mrs. Hurley said. "But with Tommy Levit running Lou's campaign, this isn't turning into boys against girls, is it?" she asked.

"Mom," groaned CJ. "Stop."

Mrs. Hurley smiled at me. She is really beautiful, like TV star beautiful, with milky skin and sparkling eyes and excellent posture. She turned to look at CJ and kept smiling, but you know how a smile that you force to stay a few seconds longer than it wants to looks a little stale? I do that, so I recognized it on Mrs. Hurley. It made me want to put my arm around her and tell her that things will work out OK for CJ, that I'm not a lousy friend, that CJ is much stronger than she seems. Weird way to feel toward a mother. I realized nobody was talking, all of us just standing there in my front hall.

I didn't want to say the wrong thing about how the election planning was going, and judging from my recent record, I was likely to. I looked for Morgan. She was sitting cocooned on the bottom step, hugging her knees. She didn't look up, so I went over and sat down next to her, and my right arm, which had been itching to go around Mrs. Hurley's shoulder, ended up on Morgan's. To my surprise, Morgan leaned against me.

"Well, 'bye," CJ mumbled.

I said good-bye but didn't stand up to walk them to the door, since Morgan was unexpectedly resting on me. Mrs. Hurley, CJ, and Olivia filed out. I wasn't sure what Morgan wanted to do, so I just sat there, waiting.

"Sorry," she said after a while, without budging.

"That's OK," I assured her. I wasn't sure what she was apologizing about.

We sat there for a while longer. My behind was getting a little cramped, but I didn't feel like I should move. I was hoping none of my sisters would need the stairs any time soon because we didn't seem near moving.

"She's always late," Morgan said a few minutes later.

"Oh, so's mine." I had to shift a little; I'm not so good at staying still. Morgan pulled away from me and leaned against the wall. She looked sad, so I added, "I'm lucky if my mother remembers to get me at all."

"I'm lucky if mine forgets me," said Morgan, flexing her bare feet.

"Mine did forget me!" I was grinning like an idiot, like this was some great thing. "Last week, first soccer practice? You'd already left. My mother forgot all about me until everybody was sitting down at dinner, and she noticed one chair was empty."

Morgan turned to look at me. "Seriously?" She smiled a tiny bit, no teeth.

"Absolutely." I shrugged. "Doesn't really bother me, though."

"Me, either." Morgan blew her long bangs out of her eyes. "Can you imagine CJ, though?"

"If her mother forgot her?"

"Not that she ever would," Morgan said quickly. "I don't think Mrs. Hurley has a non-CJ thought, ever."

I tucked my hair behind my ear.

"CJ would freak. But I think it makes us stronger. Don't you think? We're more, like, independent than CJ or Olivia."

I nodded a little, looking at my red shoelaces instead of at Morgan. "I guess," I admitted. I felt guilty talking bad about my best friend with her ex-best friend, but on the other hand Morgan had a point — in some ways, CJ and Olivia are babied much more than Morgan and me. I was thinking maybe I feel older because I have older sisters and big boobs, but maybe Morgan is right — she and I are more independent.

"You want to go up to your room?" Morgan asked.

"Sure." I was happy to get off the stairs.

When we got to my room, I spotted the red vinyl bag of jacks on my desk. I saw Morgan noticing it, too, but she quickly went over and sat down on my bed. I grabbed the bag and brought it over to her.

I was holding it there in front of her a few seconds before she reached out to take it. She seemed to be weighing it in her palm as she inspected it. "Thanks," she whispered.

"A present is a present," I said.

"Even from someone you hate." Morgan flopped down on my bed and placed the bag of jacks on her flat belly.

"My sister Colette hates my dad," I whispered.

"Really?" Morgan asked. "Your dad seems so harmless."

"Well, I don't know if she really, really hates him," I quickly explained. "My sister Anne Marie says they just press each other's buttons and that probably they love each other the most. Which makes me feel great."

Morgan turned her head to look at me, more kindly than she usually does. I shrugged to show I wasn't mortally wounded or anything, then lay down beside her on my bed, with my arms crossed under my head, and said, "I don't know. I'm not sure whether to believe Anne Marie or Colette, either. It sure sounds like hate sometimes. But then, I don't know. I don't think you can really hate your father."

"Trust me," she said. "You can." She got up and walked over to my window. "Wow, you can see right into Tommy and Jonas's yard from here."

"Yeah."

"You could totally spy on them."

"Uh-huh."

She opened her mouth wide and hit my foot lightly with her open hand. "You wicked person!"

"I know it!"

"Have you seen anything good? Tell me!"

I tried to think of something. "One time, I was out in our yard with my sisters. I guess I was really little."

She nodded.

"And, see that window up there? The little one?"

"With the yellow curtains?"

"Yeah," I said. "But there weren't curtains then because, well, we were all out there playing tag or kickball or something, and I guess I stopped and pointed at the window and said, "There's Mr. Levit. Is he pee-pee-ing?"

"No way!"

I nodded. "The yellow curtains went up that night."

"I love it!" Morgan shrieked. "You actually saw him?"

I shrugged and admitted, "I've told the story so

many times, it's hard to remember exactly what I saw."

"Just imagine if you hadn't said it so loud," Morgan whispered, clutching my arms to pull me close.

We both looked out my window and imagined. It felt naughty.

"Phew," I said.

Morgan pointed again. "That tree house still gives me the shivers."

"The kiss that shook the world," I agreed. "How hard did he kiss you?"

"Hard," Morgan said.

"Like a punch, hard?" I didn't want to seem obscenely interested in the way that Tommy had kissed her last year, but I had been wondering for a long time, trying to picture it.

"More like . . . a press." She put the heel of her hand against my chin and pushed me. "Like that."

"Oh," I said. "That must've been terrible."

"Maybe it wasn't that hard," she said, sitting down on my bed.

My knees felt wobbly, too, so I sat right down on the floor. "Because he seems like, like more of a gentle kisser." I felt myself blushing. "I don't know why. That's stupid, I guess. I've never kissed anybody, so what do I know?"

"Maybe it was gentle," Morgan whispered. "Maybe it's what you were saying, about not remembering exactly, because of telling the story so much."

"Yeah," I said.

"He's cute this year, huh?" she asked.

I nodded.

"His haircut," she said. "Could you die?"

"Yes! I can't believe — I know," I said.

She shook her head fast, like a dog getting dry. "Whew. Weird he likes CJ, though."

"What do you mean?" I asked. I don't know if she could hear my voice shivering, but it sure sounded shaky to me.

"Maybe I'm crazy." She lay back on my bed with her arms flung back past her head. "But he seems like he'd want a more independent person."

"I don't think you're crazy." I twisted the friendship ring around my finger.

"But when you asked him who he liked, he said CJ?"

"Um," I said.

Morgan sat up. "You passed him a note in Mrs. Shepard's class, I remember. Asking who he liked, right?"

"Uh-huh." I couldn't stop myself from smiling, remembering that note, remembering finding it in my hand at the end of that period, unfolding it, reading it. Remembering the way he had watched me, that whole class, with his head bent forward and his eyes focused hard on my face.

"And that afternoon he asked out CJ."

"Mmm-hmm," I admitted.

Morgan's eyes were open wide. "What am I missing?"

Don't, I thought, but there I was, crawling over to my dresser, pulling open the bottom drawer, rummaging around under my sweatshirts until I found the tightly folded piece of paper. I lifted it out and clutched it tightly in my hand.

"Is that the note?" Morgan asked.

I handed Morgan the folded paper and covered my face while she carefully unfolded it. Then I climbed up onto my bed next to her, to read the note for about the billionth time, to assure myself it really wasn't my imagination — to make certain again that, just as I remembered, there was my loopy handwriting of *Tommy Levit likes* _____ and then, in his pointy script, my name.

Tommy Levit likes <u>Zoe Grandon.</u>

It was still there, in black and white. OK, blue and white.

"Oh. My. God," Morgan said.

I scrunched my face tight, reread the note, then took it gently from her, reread it again, and forced myself to fold it carefully, to save it for another time. With my thumb I covered the *For Zoe Only* he'd written on the outside. I try to limit myself to one look at the note each day, two on weekend days.

"And after he passed you this, you fixed him up with CJ?"

I nodded, getting off the bed to put the note away. "She's my best friend," I explained. "And she liked him, so . . ."

Morgan frowned. "But Tommy wrote down that he liked you!"

As Morgan said that, Devin opened the door to our room and walked in. She stopped, still, in the middle of the room and looked from Morgan to me and back again a couple of times. "Stupid," she said. "Stupid, stupid." Then she turned around and left, closing the door quietly behind her.

twelve

Morgan's mother finally picked her up around 5:30. Devin was sitting at the kitchen table, and she didn't say a word to me or Morgan, just sat there drinking a glass of Diet Coke as Morgan and I said good-bye and Morgan's mother beeped in the driveway. After I stopped waving, I poured myself some Diet Coke and told Devin, "She's my friend, so you shut up."

"If you say so," Devin said, taking another sip.

Anne Marie came into the kitchen, jingling her car keys. "You ready, Devin?"

Devin stood up.

"Come on, come on. I have studying to do," Anne Marie coaxed her. While Devin rinsed her glass, Anne Marie asked me, "What's wrong with you?"

"Same old, same old," Devin answered for me.

"Tommy?" Anne Marie asked me.

I held out my hands. "Hey!"

"My advice?" Anne Marie asked, and then without waiting for an answer, told me, "Move on. You can't make a boy like you, you just make a fool of yourself trying."

"And Anne Marie should know," Devin said.

"You want a ride or not?"

"Kidding, kidding. Chris Boyne is a dweeb anyway."

"Shut up!" Anne Marie yelled, taking a swipe at Devin's head. Devin dodged her and grabbed her backpack. "I'm baby-sitting for you tonight, right?" Anne Marie asked me.

"I don't need a baby-sitter," I reminded her. "I'm twelve years old."

"It gives her an excuse to stay in," Devin yelled from the car. "She's moved on from Chris to baby-sitting!"

I heard Anne Marie threaten Devin that she could walk to Callie's, but they got into the car and drove away. I ate dinner with Anne Marie and then went to my room, telling Anne Marie I had to study. *I finally have the room to myself,* I wrote down on a piece of paper. I put one of my CDs in Devin's boom box and flipped through my address book, although I know pretty much everybody's number by heart. I couldn't think who I was in the mood to call. I even almost called Gabriela, but I couldn't remember which house she was at, and as awful as this sounds, I just wasn't in the mood for her upbeat attitude. I doodled for a while and went down to watch TV. Bay woke me up when she came in and told me to come upstairs. As we brushed our teeth together, she asked if I wanted her to get out the sleeping bag so I could camp out on their floor, but I told her no thanks, I was really looking forward to having the room to myself.

I got under my covers and listened to the quiet for a while. It was creepy, and I was more awake than ever, so I threw back the covers, tiptoed over to my dresser, pulled Tommy's note out of the drawer, and jumped back into bed like I'd been on some kind of spy mission. My heart was pounding. Without reading the note, I stuck it between my pillows and lay there on top. I felt like the princess and the pea. Finally, I had to pull it out and read it about a million times to fall asleep. *Tommy Levit likes Zoe Grandon.*

Sunday morning the house was weirdly quiet when I got up. Mom was at work, selling cars, because fall is a really busy season for her and Uncle Pete needs Sundays to be with Gabriela. Devin was still at Callie's, and Anne Marie drives Bay to tennis practice.

On my way to the bathroom, I knocked on the

door next to mine to see what Colette was up to. "Go away," she growled.

"It's me," I told her. We were the only two sisters home; I thought maybe she'd want to have breakfast together or something.

"Go away," she repeated.

"Did something happen?" I asked the closed door. I tried the knob, but it was locked. "Are you mad at somebody?"

The book or whatever she threw at the door felt like it was going to burst right through the wood and crack me in the jaw. I flinched, then said, "I get the hint," and went down the hall to the bathroom.

As I was brushing my teeth, I watched myself. I've been wondering lately if I'm going to turn all intense like Colette and Anne Marie, now that I'm in puberty. I have been a lot more moody lately, so it's possible. I made a wish that if that happens, I'll be more like Anne Marie. At least Mom and Dad are proud of Anne Marie. Mom says Colette will be the death of her. My conscience would not be able to handle that.

I washed my face and flopped down the stairs still in my boxers and T-shirt. Dad was lying on his back on the kitchen floor with his toolbox open and metal tools scattered around.

"Didn't you already fix that?"

Dad banged his head on the droopy pipe and screwed up his face at me. "Hand me a wrench," he said.

I handed him one of his wrenches. "What's wrong with it?"

"I'm trying to . . . I can certainly fix a — stupid — here's the . . ."

I heard him hammering the wrench against the pipe.

"Ffff," he grunted. "Hand me a . . . Zoe?"

"I'm here."

"Hand me the duct tape, huh?"

"You sure?" I looked at the almost-used-up roll of duct tape on the top of Dad's dented red toolbox. "Maybe you should use more tools instead."

"And a towel, huh?"

I handed him the roll of duct tape and the dish towel from its hook. I heard him ripping duct tape off the roll and humming with satisfaction.

I got a bowl and poured myself some cereal and milk, then glanced out the window. I have to eat really fast once the milk is in, because I can't stomach soggy cereal, but as I was shoveling a heaping spoonful into my mouth, I saw Tommy, Jonas, and Lou Hochstetter walking across the Levits' close-cropped dark green lawn toward their tree house, which actually sits on the grass right near the fence between our lawns. I have excellent vision so I could see what they were bringing out there. Oak tag.

I almost choked on my cereal. My appetite was gone, the first time in my life that ever happened. Eating was just suddenly disgusting to me. I spit out my mouthful and dumped the rest of the cereal down the disposal. Oak tag. I still hadn't gotten any oak tag for my campaign, and of course was planning not to, but just seeing Tommy with oak tag made me think of last year, of being the one out there with him and Jonas, making MY campaign posters, and I couldn't help it, I missed it. Missed making posters, and missed campaigning, and missed being the one out there in the tree house with them, working on it. I had my girlfriends, it's true, but with them lately I have to watch everything I say and everything I do. I can't just be my own obnoxious, coarse, rowdy self. I have to be so careful, it's wearing me out.

I was leaning all the way across the sink, watching the boys, wishing I could be tramping across the grass with them. Tommy looked up, then, right into my eyes. It was as if I'd called his name or something, the way he just turned his head and latched right onto my eyes, across our yards, through the window.

Caught. I didn't know what to do. My hands started

moving randomly, fast, grabbing stuff, the sponge, the steel wool — trying to grab something sturdy, I guess. Without taking my eyes from Tommy's, I latched onto the water handle. *Better wash my cereal down the drain,* I thought, and yanked the handle up.

"Zoe!" Dad yelled.

I gasped. I had totally spaced on the fact that my father was down there under the sink. "Sorry!" I yelled.

Dad slid out from the cabinet. He was soaked. I grabbed him the other dish towel and felt myself wavering between laughing and crying.

"I'm so sorry, Daddy. I forgot all about you!"

He chuckled a little. "Story of my life," he said, sopping up his dripping curly hair with the dirty towel.

By the time I looked back out the window, Tommy had disappeared into the tree house with Jonas and Lou. I sat down on the floor next to my father and picked up a hammer. "Story of my life, too," I told him.

thirteen

When I got to school Monday morning, it was drizzling. Morgan and CJ were sitting up on the wall together, with the hoods of their windbreakers up. Morgan was whispering in CJ's ear, and CJ was nodding. I waved at them and smiled. CJ looked down. Morgan looked away.

I didn't stop smiling. I started to climb up to sit on the wall with them, but the warning bell rang and they jumped down. None of us gets free breakfast, so we usually just wait for the second bell.

"Hey, guys," I said. I had forgotten my rain jacket, so I gathered my hair and twisted it, hoping to avoid frizz.

"Hi," CJ said quietly, without making eye contact.

"Tommy and Jonas had lots of posters with them," I told them. "On the bus this morning. For Lou."

"If you wanted . . . " CJ straightened her legs so tight, they looked curved backward. "We, if you want posters, we . . . "

"No," I assured her. "I don't really care. Boy, it sure is starting to rain."

Olivia wandered over to us, her umbrella up to shield her and the paperback book she was reading. She stood in front of us like that for a few seconds. Morgan, CJ, and I all waited, shrugging at one another. When Olivia lowered the book, she blinked a few times. She looked surprised to find herself in front of us, at school.

"It's raining," she mentioned.

The second bell rang and the four of us, our little clique, walked into school without talking. On the way we passed my cousin Gabriela hanging a poster on the lobby bulletin board. It was on red oak tag and it said, in blue marker, LOU IS WHO WILL DO. There were gobs of glitter in pools of dried white glue.

I didn't want to be the one to comment.

At the lockers, we all opened our combinations (except Olivia, who bent to use her key) and dumped our extra stuff in. There was a big clattering of the hollow metal being pounded by old heavy texts. CJ, Morgan, and Olivia wiggled out of their wet windbreakers. I shook myself off, slammed my locker shut, and waited; I don't like to be slow.

"Well, it rhymes," Olivia said, closing her locker gently. "But I guess Lou is an easy name to rhyme."

"Oh," CJ said. "Here." She handed me Big Blue, my favorite sweatshirt. I had given it to her the day we became best friends, after she rode her bike over to my house to tell me Tommy had asked her out. She had been sitting on my bed shivering, so I'd given her Big Blue, my most special thing in the world, and I'd felt good about it, like I had grown up, like — see, she is more important to me than anything, than any *thing*.

I didn't stretch out my hand to take it. I hadn't said I wanted it back.

"I washed it," CJ said, as if I were afraid it was dirty.

I took it, and while I redialed my combination, I smelled Big Blue. It didn't smell like Big Blue anymore. I placed it gently on the top shelf of my locker, closed the door, and jiggled the lock. Then I remembered to say, "Thanks."

I noticed I was twirling a piece of my hair, a habit I'd broken and gotten a Minnie Mouse Pez dispenser for breaking, when I was five years old. I forced my hand into my tight jeans pocket. Not that my mother would remember and take the Pez dispenser away now, as she had warned she'd do if I went back to twirling, but on principle.

Olivia pushed her lower lip away from her braces and said to me, "I'm sure your posters will be good, too."

"I don't care," I mumbled.

"Ew," screeched Morgan. "What's that?" She was pointing at the floor, where there was a liquid trail of red.

We all gasped, with the same thought in our heads. *Is somebody bleeding?* I quickly looked down at my jeans and tried to be casual about looking at my behind — all the while praying, *Please let it not be me.*

"Is it me?" Morgan asked nervously. She showed her behind. We all shook our heads.

"It can't be me," Olivia said, checking her pants to be sure, anyway. "I doubt I'll get my period before I'm sixteen."

I swallowed hard. I didn't get mine in July or August, but Devin promised me that's pretty common when you're just starting. "Is it me?" I asked nervously. I didn't feel anything, inside me, but I've only had my period five times so I'm not such an expert at all on the way it feels.

My friends looked me over.

CJ gasped.

"Oh, no," I moaned.

"No, no," CJ said, touching my arm and pointing to the floor. "It's OK. It's just your shoelaces."

We all gawked at my sneakers, with their red shoelaces dripping red puddles.

"Oh." I rested my face in my palms.

"Shoelaces," I heard one of them whisper.

"Thank goodness," I said, mostly to myself. "Thank you, thank you." I took a few breaths through my hands, breathing the smell of soap from the upstairs bathroom off them, trying to calm myself down. My whole body was shaking. "I don't know what I would've done."

CJ rubbed my arm.

"The nurse has stuff," Morgan said.

I sighed, thanking every power that might exist that I didn't have to tie Big Blue around my hips and run to the nurse. "Just my shoelaces," I mumbled into my palms.

"Why did you get red shoelaces, anyway?" Morgan asked me.

I shrugged with my hands still over my face, but then peeked out between my fingers. Morgan was looking at CJ, who took her warm hand off my arm. I checked — yes, she was still wearing her friendship ring. Thank goodness. I looked at mine. The knot had slipped down palm-side, in all the excitement. As I fixed it, I watched my hands shaking uncontrollably.

"Wow," I said to my friends. "Look at how my hands are shaking." I held them out. The three girls all looked at them.

"Shaky," Olivia commented.

"Oh," I said again, still trying to recover. I massaged my hands with each other and tried to force my shoulders back, to stand up straight. Instead I shivered. "Phew," I said. "My whole body is freaking out."

The warning bell for homeroom rang.

"What a way to start the day," I said, and tucked my hair behind my ears, the way CJ had told me looked good on me. "Ugh. Anyway."

"Anyway," repeated CJ. She stood right in front of me and looked into my eyes questioningly. I smiled at her. She didn't smile back. After a few seconds, she pivoted and walked off toward her homeroom. Morgan chased after her and left me and Olivia without saying a word.

I wiggled my friendship ring on my finger and asked Olivia, "Doesn't this ring itch?"

She shook her head. "It doesn't itch me."

"My whole body is freaking out," I said again as she and I started walking toward our homeroom. "Does that ever happen to you?"

"Not so much," she said. "But you're more advanced, in that way."

"Lucky me," I groaned. "I'll meet you. I'd better stop at the bathroom for some paper towels to dry off these stupid shoelaces."

fourteen

The only two things that got me through the rest of the day were the paper towels and the fact that there'd be no school the next day because of the Jewish New Year. I was grateful enough for the break to consider converting, but if I did, Devin would say it's just because Tommy's family is Jewish.

When I got home, I kicked off my now-pinkish sneakers with their horrible drippy laces before I was all the way through the door. A package was sitting on the kitchen table, with my name on it. I grabbed a knife and sliced off the packing tape, then rummaged through the Styrofoam and coupons to find the two packages of black pencils with neon-colored erasers. And, in gold, ZOE GRANDON FOR PRESIDENT.

They were beautiful and original, but ultimately, I guess, stupid.

I brought them up to my room and sat on my bed, looking at them for a few minutes, before I hid them in my sweatshirt drawer and put my spring-fresh-smelling Big Blue snuggly on top of them. I closed the drawer quickly. I didn't let myself look at the Tommy note that was in there, too. I wanted to save my one look for bedtime, so I dragged myself into the bathroom and, for lack of anything else to keep me from my bottom drawer, scrubbed my face.

CJ called me while we were eating dinner and said she had to talk to me. I asked if I could call her back later, and she said no — she wanted to talk in person, so could she come over in the morning? I said OK and lost my appetite again. If Dad hadn't brought home blondies from the bakery, I would've skipped dessert entirely.

After dinner, I found a new pair of plain white laces in the linen closet to put into my sneakers. I tugged out the still-damp red ones and stuck them in my sweatshirt drawer. If things keep going at this pace, my sweatshirts will have to move to the closet.

I woke up early worrying about what CJ had to talk about and was waiting on my front lawn, barefoot, before Dad even left for work. "Hiya, sweetheart," he said, holding the car door open for Elvis, who jumped in, wagging his tail. "What are you doing up and out so early?"

Before I could answer he said, "And go put on some shoes. You'll catch a cold." He got into the car and drove off, waving. If I'd been Colette, he would've yanked me into the house and slammed my sneakers onto my feet. I waved until he rounded the corner. Maybe it's easier not being loved most.

A few minutes later, a van pulled into the space Dad had left in the driveway. It was a white van with BROWN AND BROTHER, PLUMBERS on the side. I had to smile, wondering which Mr. Brown had to be just "and brother." Meanwhile, a little old man lowered himself out of the van, hoisted a huge tool belt onto his narrow hips, and limped to my back door. I sat on the lawn for a few minutes, but my curiosity overwhelmed me, so I had to go find out what he was doing in my house.

When I pulled open the door, Mom gasped. She was standing against the counter near the sink, next to Mr. Brown's (or maybe it was his brother's) legs, which jutted out from under the sink just the way Dad's had, two days before.

"I thought you were Daddy!" Mom whispered. "He forgot his wallet, of all days. Maybe I should just go bring it to him."

"Why?" I asked. "What's going on?"

She held her hand out, displaying the plumber's legs. "Daddy would kill me, but the linoleum is beginning to buckle."

"Didn't Daddy fix the sink already?"

"When your father plays Mr. Fixit, all our appliances panic."

"But . . ." I was so confused. "You always said Daddy could fix anything."

Mom smiled, as if I were a little kid just figuring out maybe one fat guy in a sleigh didn't bring presents to all the children's houses.

"That was a lie?" I asked.

Mom shrugged. "The truth is overrated."

I kneeled down beside the plumber and asked, "How does it look?"

"It ain't pretty," he answered. He inspected me with his sleepy-looking eyes for a second and then went back to his work, just as the doorknob creaked.

Mom shrieked. Poor CJ, outside the door, was clutching her heart.

I stood up and opened the door for her. "Come in. Sorry," I said. "We're just a little jumpy because the plumber is here."

"Oh," said CJ, tiptoeing into the room, looking at the plumber's legs.

I opened the fridge and chose two apples. CJ had to

lower her hand from her neck, where it was nervously rubbing, to take her apple. She polished the apple on her sweatshirt. The apple had been washed already; my mom does it before she puts them in the fridge. I wouldn't have given her a dirty apple.

CJ leaned close to whisper in my ear, "The plumber makes you jumpy?"

"We thought you might be my dad."

"Uh-huh," CJ said.

"My dad fixed the sink, Sunday, but apparently . . . "

"Oh," CJ said, relaxing. She slid gracefully into one of the kitchen chairs. "My dad fixed the sink once. We had to renovate the whole kitchen."

"Don't even tell me that," Mom said.

"I thought my dad could fix anything," I mumbled.

"Time you learned," Mom groaned, slumping into the chair next to CJ.

I was shrugging at CJ like it was no big deal, finding out the truth about my dad and having to rearrange my whole image of him, when Mom sprang up suddenly like she'd sat on fire. "What was that?"

"I didn't hear . . . " I started. Then I heard a car door slam. I ran over and looked out the kitchen window. "Dad!"

"Down in the basement," Mom ordered. She raced to the basement door and whipped it open. The plumber stood up and, without gathering his tools, limped toward the basement door Mom was holding open impatiently. He was halfway across the kitchen when I saw the top of Dad's head through the window. The plumber was moving in slow motion. He was, like, a hundred years old, and my mother looked ready to pick him up by the belt loops and toss him down the basement stairs any second. "Zoe!" Mom yelled. "Show him. Now!"

CJ and I ran for the basement. Mom started tossing tools under the sink. I closed the basement door behind the plumber just as the back door opened. In the dark of the stairwell, CJ, the plumber, and I could hear Mom telling Dad, "No, I was just looking at the repairs you made. Seems to be holding."

Dad said something that ended with "duct tape."

The plumber mumbled, "Yeah, his duct tape."

I put my hand over the plumber's mouth and held him still. He was my height but very bony, like a bird — fragile-looking, which made me feel guilty for manhandling him, but I wasn't taking any chances. And he had no right saying anything about my father. I wanted that to be very clear to him.

After no sound for a few seconds, CJ whispered, "Where's the light?"

The plumber was looking at me so pathetically, and

his mouth area was so prickly, I let go of him. "Shh," I whispered to him. He stayed quiet. "In the kitchen," I whispered to CJ.

CJ started to laugh silently. I did, too. I sat down on the step, and the plumber sat down beside me. He lifted his tool belt to avoid making a clatter.

"You must think we're lunatics," I whispered to him.

"You'd be surprised how many basements I've been shoved into," he said.

"Really?"

He shrugged, slowly, and grumbled, "Occupational hazard."

I offered him a bite of my apple. Maybe that's unsanitary but I felt bad. Here CJ and I both had a snack; he had a wrench. Anyway, he said no thanks.

We were sitting there in cozy silence when the door flew open. I looked up into the bright of the kitchen to see my father looming there hugely.

"Hi, Dad."

"Who's this?" Dad demanded.

"CJ Hurley," I said.

"Hi," said CJ, her apple still mid-bite in her mouth.

"I meant the other one," Dad enunciated.

"I'm the plumber," said the plumber. He stood up and extended his hand for Dad to shake just as Mom grabbed Dad's arm.

"Arnie," she pleaded.

"Hon," he said calmly, turning to Mom. "Have you met Zoe's friends? This is CJ and this is the plumber."

"Yes," Mom said. "We've met." But the plumber had moved his open hand toward Mom, so she shook it.

"You kids keep playing. Didn't mean to interrupt," Dad said sweetly, and slammed the door hard in our faces. CJ, the plumber, and I stood there in the dark, listening to the silence on the other side of the door.

After about a minute, the plumber said, "Well, that's a new one."

"Have you been here before?" I asked the plumber. He nodded. "Wow," I whispered. "That's so weird. My mom has been just lying, all this time."

CJ finished biting and said, "I think it's sweet, she wanted to protect him. His feelings, I mean. Don't you?"

"Sure. Well, I think it's funny," I said, tucking my hair behind my ears. The plumber sat down again on the step and fiddled with his wrench. "Sorry about this," I told him.

He folded his crinkly hands in his lap and said, "I get paid by the hour."

CJ propped her leg up on the banister and calmly ate her apple. They both seemed perfectly relaxed, like this was a completely normal situation, the three of us trapped in the dark basement stairwell. Meanwhile, I was developing a major case of claustrophobia. After another minute, I couldn't take it anymore. I needed some air. I opened the door a crack and looked around. Mom and Dad were both gone. "Phew," I breathed. "Ahh." I held open the door to let CJ and the plumber out.

The plumber limped back to the sink, opened the cabinet underneath, and, knees cracking, got down on the floor and back underneath. CJ smiled at me. "Better?"

I nodded.

"Because there's, I have, there's something I . . . "

"Let's go up to my room," I suggested.

"Mmm-hmm." She took a deep breath, lifted her chin, and tiptoed up the stairs ahead of me.

fifteen

CJ pulled four boxes of pencils and a Sharpie marker out of the front pocket of her sweatshirt. She placed them on my bed, then sat down in a wide straddle on my floor and looked up at me.

I closed my door. "What?" I asked her. I sat down on the floor against the door and pulled my knees in to my chest, to rest my chin on.

"It was a good idea. It was original and very — you."

"Pencils?"

"Zoe for president."

I grinned big. "I was just kidding."

"You haven't done anything. You could lose, you know."

"Oh," I said, totally relieved. "Is that what you're worried about? I don't even care. So what if I do lose? It's no big deal to me."

"Don't lie."

"No, no. I guess I'm just growing out of always having to win. I'm over it."

CJ stretched her body in front of her legs and laid her head down on my rug. She looked like a capital T.

"Oh, my goodness," I said. "Tell me that doesn't kill."

"It hurts," she answered softly. "But in a good way."

"Whatever that means. To me, pain is pain, and I'm, like, if I can avoid it . . . " I was talking loud and fast, but I couldn't stop myself.

She lifted just her head to look at me. "That's not the kind of person I thought you were," she said, and lowered her head to my rug.

"No," I protested. "I just — it was a joke. I was kidding."

She pulled her body up to sitting again. I could just watch her stretch all day, it's really beautiful. "You're always kidding, I guess," she said sadly.

"CJ . . . "

CJ's legs moved slowly toward each other, in front of her. When they met, she grabbed her ankles. "Did Tommy want to ask you out, instead of me?"

"What are you . . . "

"Tell me," she insisted quietly.

"Why would he? What . . . if, if he, what, why?"

"Why did you fix him up with me, if you knew he liked you?" CJ's big green eyes were wet with tears. "Was it to convince me to quit dance?"

"No," I told her. "Absolutely not!"

"But he did like you."

"No," I said. "He obviously . . . He never would have visited *me* after every class, all week." I tried to smile reassuringly.

"I don't know what to think." CJ held the sides of her head with her hands, like she was trying to keep it from exploding. "Morgan said he wrote you a note, you have a note from him, that he liked you."

"Oh," I said, because it was all I could manage.

"Is it true?"

"When did Morgan . . . "

"Is it true?"

I lifted my eyes to meet hers and I lied. "No."

CJ let out a big breath and lay down in a ball on my rug.

"CJ," I pleaded. I can't handle people crying, especially when it's my fault. She wasn't making any sounds, but her back was heaving up and down, up and down. "CJ," I said again. I crawled over and rubbed her back gently.

"Why did Morgan do that to me?" she asked, into my floor.

I just groaned. What a mess I'd made for myself. I patted her on the back and walked over to my window. Nobody was out in the Levits' yard.

"I'm sorry," CJ sobbed. "I should know you'd never betray me. I'm the worst friend, thinking you, that you, of all . . ."

"Shh," I said.

She kept crying.

"Shh," I tried again, from against the wall.

"I don't want to shush," she screeched, all red-faced.

I was scared. "OK," I said quickly. "You don't have to, you go ahead, I just meant, I just wanted to make it better."

She sobbed.

"Tell me what you want me to do," I said. "And I'll do it. You want to make campaign pencils?" I picked up a handful of them, hopefully. "That's fine. We could make the pencils, if you want to. Let's do that."

"No," CJ said. She sat up and wiped her face with her palm. "I didn't realize you were joking, is all. I thought you just, you, Morgan can be so — but I should remember, you're way stronger than me. You wouldn't give in to her."

I placed the pencils gently on my bed.

"If you don't really want to be president . . . " CJ said, but interrupted herself by sneezing.

I reached to get her a tissue from the box on Devin's dresser, but something caught my eye outside. The Levits were leaving their house to go to services for the Jewish New Year. Tommy and Jonas were both wearing navy blazers, white shirts, red-and-blue ties, and gray slacks. Tommy's hair was slicked back. I gripped the windowsill for support.

"What?"

"Your boyfriend," I forced myself to say.

She stood up and came over next to me, to peek. "Wow," she said. "They look so . . . wow."

"They hate dressing alike," I told her, to keep my knees from buckling or my mouth from finishing her thought. *They look so . . . gorgeous.*

Tommy was walking around to the far car door. Out of habit I prayed for him to look up and see me. He didn't. Which is probably for the best. After they drove away, I was able to release the windowsill and pull out a tissue for CJ.

"Thanks," she said, using it. "Of all people, I, you know I think, if you don't really, really in your heart want to do all the work to do something, to try to be a star, nobody should make you. You understood that when I . . . You've been so supportive of me, quitting ballet. I didn't mean to . . . You deserve . . ."

"It's not the same. If you went back to it," I said, staring out the window to avoid looking at her. "I mean, president of seventh grade — who cares? But I would think it's great, actually, if you wanted to go back to ballet, even if it meant we couldn't hang out as much — you'd still be my best friend. You have talent, CJ. It would never come between us."

"So do you," she said. "You have talents, too."

"Yeah, right," I said. "Name one." I don't know why but all of a sudden I almost started to cry myself.

"You make people feel good about themselves," she whispered.

"Ooo, there's a talent." I opened my eyes wide to keep them from leaking tears. "I'm also — prompt! As long as we're listing my amazing qualities. Hooray for talented Zoe, cheerful and prompt."

"It is a talent," she insisted. "Everybody wants to, that's why, everybody wants to be friends with you. You listen, and you care, and you, you're a good, you know how to . . ."

"Maybe I used to." I sat down on my bed. "Lately I just piss people off."

She smiled. "No. You just don't want to run for president."

I rested my face in my palms and listened to her quiet voice.

"I, certainly, I understand, if you, a person . . . It's more comfortable, blending in with the crowd." She took a deep breath. She usually doesn't say too much in a row. "Right? I just, I never thought you — but that's fine. I knew something was making you act all tense and weird. Now I know what."

"Well, actually . . . " I started, lifting my damp face.

"I'm glad we —" She stopped herself. "What? What did you want to say?"

"Nothing," I lied.

sixteen

"That's why I said you were stupid," Devin told me, shaking a bottle of red nail polish. "Didn't you ever hear the expression, 'Three can keep a secret — if two are dead'?"

I shook my head. "No."

She grabbed my foot. "Hand me the paper towels."

I handed her the roll. She pulled off a few sheets and coiled them into a tight rope, which she laced over one toe, under the next, all the way down to my pinkie toe, which she went around, and headed back up to the big toe again, over-under. "Ouch," I said. "My pinkie toe doesn't like being separated from everybody else."

"Sounds like somebody I know," Devin said, and shook the polish again.

I looked at my toes and imagined them as the five of us. The big toe – Anne Marie, all serious and separate, independent. Next, Bay, bumpy and callused, and taller than the rest. Then Colette — well, my middle toe looks straight and calm, not like Colette at all — the opposite, actually. And then the ring toe, if that's what you call it, pretty and perfect, just like Devin. And the pinkie toe, which would be me, I guess, hiding behind and clinging to the big-sister toes, in physical agony at being separated from them and looking weirdly misshapen, alone.

Devin twisted off the top of the polish bottle.

"I'm such a pinkie toe," I admitted.

"Keep still," Devin said. She held my foot tight and delicately painted some bright red polish onto my pinkie toenail. "There," Devin said, looking at it. "Not bad. Better, right?"

I shrugged. It did look sort of cute. "So now what do I do?"

"Hold still." She moved on to the next toe. "Well, you can wear my clogs to school tomorrow. How awful. You poor thing. Why did you ever insist on those red shoelaces? I told you they were stupid."

"I know. I just thought they were, I don't know, different."

"That they were," Devin agreed. "Wear my clogs. Then you can slip them off and people will see your toes. Look how much prettier, how much more feminine they look. You have the hugest big toenail I ever saw."

"I do?" I looked. She was right. I'd never noticed before. "Great. Another reason to hate myself. Terrific. So what do I do about the note?"

"Just avoid the topic," Devin advised. "No reason to go looking for trouble. And anyway, it's nobody's business but your own. Give me your other foot."

The next morning I put on Devin's clogs. It was hard to keep them on. By the time I got downstairs to breakfast, my toes were exhausted from gripping them. "Don't forget," Devin reminded me as she was racing out the door after our older sisters.

"Be where he might go," I said. "I know, I know." She'd only drilled me a hundred times while my toes were drying. *Be where he might go, so he'll have to cross your path. Ask him a question. Play dumb.* For the first time I could understand why Colette always acts so angry about schoolwork, because of her learning disability. I think I have a flirting disability. Devin is naturally gifted. It's enough to make me really jealous, if she weren't so nice to me sometimes.

Jonas passed me, running for the bus. *Clomp, clomp,* I went, trying to hurry in the clogs. The bus was already there. I could see it up ahead, could see Jonas racing up the steps and the door closing. I tried to run but when I lifted my foot, the left clog fell off and I had to go back for it. *Tsss*, went the bus, and I looked up to see the back end of it moving away from me, down the street, toward school.

I dropped my books and cursed, then picked them up again and began the long clomp to school, where I got a late slip. So much for being prompt. And I already had a huge blister on one of my middle toes. *Turns out it's not so opposite from Colette,* I thought as I inspected it during the math quiz I think I bombed.

Fourth period, I got to the lockers after my friends had already left for the cafeteria. I hustled to put myself in the route Tommy would be taking, but I guess I was too slow because when I finally gave up and headed in for lunch, I noticed him finishing up his sandwich at the boys' table.

I clomped toward my friends, noticing how incredibly huge the cafeteria was. Such a long way to go when you're walking thighs first and concentrating on not littering your footwear along the way. Tommy was shooting his brown bag toward the garbage can. By instinct I lunged for it and caught it. Just as the bag hit my palm, I thought, *Oops.* I dropped it and swung my hair over my face, looked at Tommy, then flicked my eyes down and away.

The only problem was, the whole move was really hard to coordinate on its own, but adding the additional challenges of the walk and the clogs — well, anyway, I stepped on Tommy's lunch bag, turned my ankle, and nearly wiped out. One clog went skittering across the floor toward the boys' table, and I only kept the rest of myself off the floor by amazing willpower and a big stumble into the garbage can. I braced myself on the edges, then quickly limped over to get the missing clog. "Call me Grace," I mumbled toward the boys, but kept my hair in front of my face. With one clog in my hand and one on a foot, I hobbled over to my friends.

"We're done," Morgan told me. I brought my lunch and my clog with me and clomped along after them toward the exit. *So much for cheerful, too,* I was thinking.

"I'll prove it to you," I heard Morgan yell to CJ, ahead of me.

Morgan stomped over to me. "What did the note say?"

"What note?" I stopped in the doorway. Tommy, Jonas, Gideon, and Lou Hochstetter were bunched up behind me. I glared at Morgan, daring her.

Morgan blew the bangs out of her eyes and crossed her arms angrily. "The note that said *Tommy Levit likes Zoe Grandon!*"

I shook my head a little. I felt so betrayed and so ashamed at the same time. CJ was standing behind Morgan, her fingers nervously touching her hair. *She deserves better than me or Morgan,* I thought, and wishing to disappear, turned my face away from them. Unfortunately, that brought me eye to eye with Tommy. His eyes were bloodshot and squinting. All the boys were staring at him. Tommy spun around and went back into school, with all the boys chasing after him.

"I don't know what you're talking about," I said, toward Morgan's feet.

"You're lying!" Morgan yelled, and shoved me. I'm a pretty solid person but I wasn't expecting that and also I was off-balance, with one bare foot, so I toppled backward onto my butt. I dropped my clog, my lunch, and my books.

Morgan stepped over me and disappeared down the corridor. I reached out to grab CJ's and Olivia's extended hands, and pulled myself up.

"I can't believe her," CJ asked. "Are you hurt?"

"Me?" I asked, brushing off my behind and trying to force out a laugh. "With all this padding, how could I get hurt?"

seventeen

Nobody talked to anybody, much, the rest of the day. Tommy somehow managed to develop a fever, the lucky, and got sent home sick by the nurse. Not a single person passed me a note in English/social studies, so I was forced to actually pay attention in class. I even managed to finish up my independent work independently, and early enough to look up all my vocab words. If I hadn't been feeling so thoroughly disgusted with myself, I might've been proud.

Soccer practice was terrible. My blister had popped and was oozing inside my soccer sock, and my body felt all loose and bouncy. I was completely grossing myself out. Coach Cress benched me. She was right to. When the late bus left me off, I walked home barefoot, unable to bear the clogs another step. I left them under Devin's bed and pulled out my sneakers with their bright white shoelaces, but that depressed me, so I threw them in my closet, slammed the closet door, and went in my socks straight to the den, to sit down and veg out in front of the TV. Anne Marie was reading a book in the recliner where Bay usually sits. I picked up the clicker but nothing happened. I tried a few times but nothing.

Without raising her head from the book, Anne Marie explained, "Dad fixed the VCR."

I had to smile, my first smile of the day. "Does Mom know?"

Anne Marie nodded. "You didn't hear them screaming this morning?"

I shook my head. "Really screaming?"

"I wouldn't go upstairs. Their door is closed."

"Great," I said. Mom and Dad behind closed doors meant either fighting or making up, and we all knew enough to keep clear of both. I lay down with my arm over my face and my feet up on the back of the couch and just felt sad.

Dinner ended up being fend-for-yourself, and afterward I sat at the table with my sisters and for lack of anything better, actually did my homework. I had to write a short story starting with the first sentence, "I knew nothing would ever be the same the minute I saw it." I made "it" be a bag of jacks that arrived in the mail, imagining that Mom and Dad never resolved this fight, so they got divorced, and one day a bag of jacks showed up in the mail, and I looked at it and realized my dad would never come back. I was almost crying while I wrote, but then I went back and crossed out everyplace I had written *bag of jacks* and put a question mark. I would have to think of a different thing a dad might send, in case my story got chosen to go up on the bulletin board. It wouldn't be fair to Morgan to put jacks. *Maybe marbles,* I was thinking when I heard footsteps on the stairs and craned my neck to see which one of them was coming.

Both.

Mom and Dad came into the dining room holding hands. "What's going on in here?" Mom asked.

"Who are you people and what have you done with our daughters?" Dad asked.

Without raising her eyes from her doodles, Devin asked, "Where are you guys going?"

Mom adjusted the clip on her hair and pursed her lips. "Sears," Dad said. "We need a new TV."

"And some duct tape," added Mom. Dad pinched her on the behind. She slapped his hand and said,

"Fresh." Then she pinched him back and ran away from him. He chased her through the kitchen and out the door. We could hear her giggling all the way out to the car. When the motor started up, the five of us had to laugh. Partly from relief, I think.

"Making up is so much better than fighting," I said. Bay and Anne Marie made eye contact and sort of smirked. "What?" I asked, but they wouldn't say a thing. I decided not to care. I know I'm right. I saw how Mom and Dad looked at each other, and it got me to thinking. I closed my books and went upstairs to have some private time, so I could make my new plan.

The next morning, I was up so early I got the first shower and was ready for school before Devin even got out of bed, my white shoelaces looking glow-in-the-dark in my now blotchy pink sneakers, but I had my game face on by then, so they truly didn't bother me anymore.

I walked to the bus stop with my sisters without saying a word and waved good-bye as the high school bus pulled away. I sat down on my books. A few minutes later, Tommy showed up. *Here we go,* I said to myself, and after a deep breath said softly to Tommy, "Beat you again."

He barely blinked.

"Joke," I whispered. Then I swallowed and told myself, *Now.* "Tommy? I'm really sorry. I know you wrote *For Zoe Only* and I never should've . . ."

He spat on the road.

"I never . . . " I stood up. "I was wrong to . . . "

"I thought we were friends," he said. His left eye twitched. His hand went up to his face, to close the lid.

"We are friends," I told him.

"No. We're not." He rubbed his eye roughly. "How could you?"

I shook my head. This wasn't exactly how I planned it. He was supposed to listen to the whole thing. "I guess . . . "

"Forget it." He watched his untied high-tops.

"I wanted someone to know you actually liked me for a second," I blurted out. Then I covered my face with my hands. I hadn't planned on admitting that. In fact, I hadn't known that was why I really had shown Morgan the note, until I heard my own voice saying so.

"I don't like you," Tommy said.

I sat back down on my books and rested my head-holding hands on my knees. I just sat there like that for a minute. I heard the bus, way up the hill, then, so I pulled myself together to finish what I'd planned to say. Without taking my eyes off my bright white shoelaces, I said, "I know saying I'm sorry is meaningless, but I am sorry. I know you probably hate me now, but I want to know if there's anything I can do to make you stop hating me."

"No," he said.

The bus was coming toward us from one direction and Jonas was running toward us from the other, so I had to hurry. "Honestly, anything. Do you want me to lose the election? That's why I haven't even made a single poster — I want you to win. Lou, I mean. I'm rooting for you, is what I mean. I don't even care about the election. That's why I haven't done anything — I want to lose, if that's what it takes. I don't care the slightest bit about winning anything. I just want everybody to like me and not be mad at me."

"Oh," Tommy said in his nastiest voice. "There's an impressive ambition."

The bus doors folded open, and Tommy climbed up. I followed right after him and, ignoring the letter and the spirit of all Devin's flirting lessons, plopped my body down next to Tommy's.

"That seat is saved for Jonas," he said.

I didn't get up. Jonas sat down next to my cousin Gabriela, who gathered her books together nervously to make room. Tommy slid as close to the window as he could without leaving the bus.

I scrunched down on my half of the seat and whispered to Tommy, "I denied the note. Nobody but Morgan knows. And Devin."

"Devin, too?"

"Well, yeah."

"Why don't you just take out an ad?"

I smiled a tiny bit. *I like him so much.* "Sorry."

He shook his head and looked away from me. "You used to be such a great person," he whispered. "Funny. Honest. Real."

"I'm still real," I bargained, pinching my own arm to prove it. "See?"

"No." He glared at me instead of smiling back. "Now you're all bendy and whispery, just like any other girl."

"Bendy?"

He tilted his head the way Devin had taught me to and looked so ridiculous imitating me, I almost could've laughed. But not quite.

eighteen

Lou's posters were everywhere. I congratulated him on them. He thanked me. He didn't ask if I was planning to start campaigning, I think because he's just a really nice guy. I complimented him again, and he blurted, "Well, I really would like to win." Then he blushed and said, "Well, I'm sure you would, too. I'm sure your posters will be great, too, last year your posters were great, so if you put up posters . . . see you in math."

We were standing right outside the math class. I followed him in the door and said, "You're right!"

Lou laughed, a big loud guffaw of a laugh. He was pretty much the only one in the grade who seemed the slightest bit happy.

Morgan wasn't talking to anybody, and CJ, convinced that Morgan was a liar, wasn't talking to her. Morgan wasn't wearing her friendship ring, I noticed. I couldn't tell whose side Olivia was on — she was walking alongside Morgan between periods but at lunch she sat with Lou. CJ was sort of talking to me, but I was having a hard time looking her in the eye, which made it difficult to have any sort of conversation. We all did homework at lunch. Mrs. Shepard looked surprised, Friday, when she returned our vocab quizzes — everybody had done really well. She said, "I don't know what's going on, but I hope it will continue."

"I hope not," I mumbled to myself.

I didn't get called on in band — it was an eighth grader named Sylvia who did her scales perfectly on the oboe, the only instrument that sounds more congested than mine. I had my clarinet in pieces before the bell rang and was one of the first kids on the bus. I sat in the front seat for the first time ever. Gabriela sat down next to me.

"Are you going to make posters this weekend?" she asked me, grinning encouragingly.

I shook my head. "Yours look good," I told her. She was the only person running for secretary, because nobody else wanted the job at all, but she had put up a few very pretty posters, anyway. "You have nice handwriting."

She smiled. "Thanks."

I looked out the window for a while, then rested my forehead on it, thankful for the cold, and closed my eyes. I could've fallen asleep, but my cousin tapped me on the shoulder and asked, "Are you OK?"

I sat up quickly and said, "Sure," in a louder voice than I'd meant. "I'm always OK."

"I know," Gabriela said. "Runs in the family. Your stop."

I looked out the window. She was right. I grabbed my books and yelled thanks to her as I hurried down the aisle and off the bus. Tommy and Jonas had run ahead. Even though I was in my white-shoelaced sneakers instead of clogs, and even though my blister had pretty much hardened into a callus, I didn't try to catch up to them. They didn't look back for me, anyway.

When I finally reached home, Bay was stretching out on the walk. "Come for a run?" she asked.

I used to beg her to take me with her on runs. Last year, I even woke up early with her a few times, and it was great because on a run is really the only time Bay chats. But I said, "No thanks."

"Why not?" she asked.

"Don't feel like it."

"Lazy," she said, her worst insult.

"No," I protested. "Busty."

"So what?" Bay asked. "So am I."

"They bounce when I run. I might give myself a black eye."

"You don't need to quit running," Bay said. "You need a sports bra. Come on, you can have one of mine." She went into the house. I followed her up to her room and sat on her bed while she rummaged through her top drawer. "Here." She threw a purple sports bra at me. "Go change. I'll wait downstairs. Hurry up, don't be pokey, Pokey."

She left me there in her room. I took off my shirt and unhooked my own bra and started yanking her sports bra down over my arms onto my chest. It felt like it was going to rip the sensitive parts of me right off as I tugged it into place. Once it was on, everything was smooshed against my rib cage. I jumped up and down a few times, to test it. Not bad; no bounce. I pulled my T-shirt back on and ran into my own room, dumped my books on my bed, and ripped off my jeans to put on some shorts. I shoved my feet back into my sneakers and ran, unbouncing, down the stairs.

Bay's feet were crossed, and she was draped over her legs. I sat on the step to tie my white laces.

"Ready?"

"Yeah," I said.

We started running. She's fast, but I kept up.

"How's the election going?" Bay asked as we passed the bus stop.

"Great," I huffed. *Yeah, great,* I was thinking. *I won't even get my own vote. Nobody likes me anymore. Nobody, nobody,* I started thinking. *I am nobody. That could be a great campaign. Vote for Nobody. Nobody likes you. Nobody cares about your problems.* Those would be excellent posters. *Nobody will work for you. Nobody for president. Nobody is your friend.*

"What's so funny?" Bay asked.

"Huh?"

"You were laughing."

I laughed and shook my head.

"Hey, what happened to your red shoelaces?"

"Don't ask."

"They were so cute. So Zoe."

"Yeah?" I looked down at my sneakers, a blur under me, with their bright white laces. "These are boring, huh?"

I picked up the pace. Bay kept up with me, then pulled ahead a little. *No way,* I thought, and pumped harder. My eyes were tearing, but a smile, a real one, spread on my mouth. Bay and I were in a flat-out sprint, both trying our hardest to win, and though my lungs were on fire, it felt terrific.

nineteen

I woke up Saturday morning knowing what I had to do.

I lay in bed for about half an hour, because I didn't want to do it.

Finally, I had to go to the bathroom, so I got up and rushed down the hall. When I was done, I flushed, and true to my recent luck, the toilet was clogged. I was afraid if I reflushed I'd flood the whole bathroom, so I yelled, "Dad!"

I stood there waiting, staring at the toilet, until it dawned on me, *The plunger is right there. If Dad comes in, he'll bring his toolbox and duct tape.* I grabbed the plunger and, well, plunged. The toilet made some obscene noises and then drained itself. I held my breath and flushed. It worked.

Dad knocked on the door. "Somebody call me?"

I yelled, "No!" and washed my hands, thinking maybe I wouldn't be a baker after all, or President. Grandon and Sister, plumbers. And I'd be Grandon.

I had showered at night after my run with Bay, but I took another. To stall. When I was dried off and dressed in Big Blue for luck, and after I'd eaten a big breakfast with the whole family except dieting Colette, I decided I couldn't put it off anymore. I dialed CJ's number and asked her if I could come over.

"You brought the pencils," CJ said happily when I pulled them out of the bag in my bike's rattrap. "Come on in. I was thinking we could, if you want, write ZOE 4 PREZ, you know, with a number four, you get it?"

I nodded, following her into her big, clean house.

"If you want," she added. "Or, or maybe, are you just returning them? Because you can keep them."

"Hi, Mrs. Hurley," I said. She was sitting on a stool that was painted to look like a cow, reading a book. She smiled nervously at me as we passed through, on our way to the stairs. I followed CJ up. Our footsteps were silent on the thick tan carpeting.

CJ closed her door and sat in a straddle on her rug. I looked around her pretty pink room, with its neat shelves of books and stuffed animals and all its ballet posters hung in frames evenly spaced along the wall. I sat down on the stool of her frilly dressing table and swiveled to face her. "CJ," I said.

I guess she could hear something in my voice, because she took her time, tilting her head up to look at me.

"I never had a best friend before you," I told her. I watched my friendship ring as the fingers on my other hand adjusted it, centered the knot exactly. "I lied to you. There is a note, I have a note, and it's exactly what Morgan said, and when I said no, I was lying."

I don't know what she was doing because my eyes were closed. I tried to finish quickly because I was pretty sure she would want me out of her house fast. "But here's the thing, CJ. I didn't fix him up with you so you would quit dance. I fixed you up because you liked him, and I just wanted to be a good friend to you. I wanted to be a best friend to you, and you wanted him, so I would do anything . . . and I lied about it because, well, at the time it felt like the right thing to do, like, I didn't want you to feel like second choice, which you aren't, you'd never be."

"Yes, I was," she said slowly. "He wanted you."

"I don't know what Tommy wanted. All I know is I wanted you for my best friend, and that's more important to me than anything, even the truth."

She breathed out hard. I didn't have the courage to look up at her if I was going to make it through all of what I needed to say. "But, CJ — here's the other thing I haven't been completely honest with you about — I think you should dance. You're a ballerina. I mean, of course, it's your decision and you have to want to do it and I'm sure it's boring sometimes, but CJ, even if you never make primo ballerina, I just think you should do what you love, and I would never, ever scheme against you."

"Prima," CJ said.

I opened my eyes. "What?"

"Prima ballerina. You said primo. It's prima." CJ was digging her fingers into her carpet, pulling up little specks of dirt, and collecting them in a pile on her sweatpants.

"Sorry. Prima."

She sniffed, and then raised her face to look at me again. "So did he ever like me?" she asked.

"I think he does now," I told her.

She lowered her head and went back to picking specks from her rug.

"Have you talked to Morgan?"

"No," I admitted. "Not yet."

"She'll never forgive you."

"I know. Will you?"

She adjusted the friendship ring on her finger. And then, slowly, she nodded.

twenty

"Morgan?"

There was silence on the other end of the phone. For a second I was happy — *I guess she recognized my voice.* I snapped out of it fast, though.

"Don't hang up," I said. I looked across the room to where CJ sat, straddling her desk chair, watching me. I switched ears and started again. "Morgan?"

"What." More of a statement than a question.

I sat down on CJ's bed and said, "You have every right to be mad at me."

She sort of snorted, like, *You bet I do.*

"Although I did show that note to you in secret," I added without quite meaning to, but that snort really annoyed me. "So in a way I have a right to be mad at—"

"You lied!" she yelled. I held the phone away from my head a little. "The whole school is calling me a liar when it's you who lied! You looked CJ in the face. 'There is no note,' you said, right to her face, knowing it was a total lie!"

"Morgan," I said, in as calming a voice as I could manage.

"I'm not talking to you until you tell CJ you lied!" She slammed the phone down so hard it sounded like breaking glass.

"She hung up," I told CJ.

CJ nodded. "She always does. Hit redial."

My finger was shaking on the redial button. Morgan picked up on the second ring and growled, "Hello."

"I told CJ," I said quickly. I waited, watching CJ sit completely still.

"Told her what?" Morgan asked.

"Told her I lied, and I told her why, and I told her I'm sorry. Which is what I want to tell you, too."

No response again.

"So, I'm sorry."

I shrugged at CJ, who was still watching me with a blank expression on her bony, pale face.

"Morgan?" I thought maybe she'd hung up again.

"What did CJ say?"

"Um," I said. "She's angry at me. She's here. You want to talk to her?"

"She's at your house?" Morgan sounded more furious than ever.

"I'm here," I said. "At hers. Hold on." I held the phone toward CJ and whispered that Morgan wanted to talk to her.

"Hi," CJ whispered into the phone. Does she say *Hi* to me like that, so confidential and soft? I slipped down, onto her floor, and pressed my back against her bed as I watched her listen to whatever Morgan was saying. I could hear the muffled sound of Morgan's voice but not her words. I layered my hands on top of my knees and propped my head there.

"I know," CJ whispered slowly. "I should have believed, uh-huh. I know."

She closed her eyes, listening. Her skin is so see-through, you could trace the map of veins in her eyelids.

"No," she said suddenly, loud and clear. "That is not why." Her eyes were open and staring at me. I shook my head, knowing what Morgan was telling her. But as lousy a person and friend as I might be, as bumbling and dishonest and bendy — I would never have fixed her up with Tommy just to get her to quit ballet. Not for nothing, but I'm actually in love with the boy. And anyway, I know we just got to be best friends recently, me and CJ, and that I've probably wrecked it, but even if she won't be my friend anymore, I won't ever stop wanting the best for her. I really won't.

She had no reason to trust me, but she said into the phone again, "No."

When I closed my eyes, they were damp with tears.

"OK," CJ was saying. "Here." She handed the phone to me.

"Hello?" I asked.

"Hello," Morgan said.

We breathed over the phone like that for a minute. I didn't know what to say next, but I didn't want to make a joke or hang up. I guess she didn't, either.

twenty-one

Sunday morning I opened my bottom dresser drawer to find my ZOE GRANDON FOR PRESIDENT pencils and on the way found my crazy red shoelaces. I pulled them out of the drawer and thought, *I like them.*

As I was stringing them back into my sneakers, I tried to think up a speech. Maybe I could even talk about the red shoelaces. *I promise, if you elect me president, I will make my mark just like these red . . .*

Nah. I pulled out three of the black pencils with their gold print, perfect and shiny, and the neon erasers — they looked great. And maybe it was important to come clean to my friends, as long as I was starting this whole honesty kick — tell them I ordered these pencils the day I was nominated, and that no matter what anybody else thought, in my opinion it was a fun, cool idea.

Nah. The truth is overrated, as Mom said.

Anyway, the pencils CJ and I had spent the afternoon making — well, they weren't as perfect, but they looked good. They looked like cooperation, at least. ZOE 4 PREZ. Nothing wrong with that. I put all the black pencils from the catalog back in my drawer. Maybe I'll run again next year or in college or sometime and be happy to have these then. When I'm mature enough to deal.

Zoe Grandon — the write choice. Maybe if I'd left myself some time to do some posters, I could use that. If I call Gabriela, I bet she'd come with me to buy some oak tag, and she might be able to draw a pencil on the poster — it could be a theme: When it comes time to write down your vote, I hope you'll . . .

Nah.

I wandered down the hall to the bathroom, to find the nail polish remover. As pretty as my toenails might be, I had decided to go back to the old Zoe. The new one was just too much trouble. I got the bottle of remover and a handful of cotton balls and went back to my room, watching my bare feet along the way. *They do look cute,* I had to admit to myself — especially those little pinkie toes, with their dots of red polish. I sat down on the floor and doused a cotton ball with the public-restroom-smelling remover. But when I was about to erase the polish, I waited a second. I splayed my toes out and looked at them, one last time, all feminine and pretty.

I clomped down the hall again. *Something on me may as well be feminine,* I told myself, and threw out the wet cotton ball. *Maybe that's good,* I decided, smiling at my toes. *Polished toenails could be a start, and I'll just need to go more gradually into girliness.* But as I was putting the bottle of polish remover away, I realized, *Wait, no, Tommy thinks feminine is bad — get rid of the polish.* I was practically paralyzed, whispering, *Decide,* to myself in the mirror.

twenty-two

I sat on the cold metal folding chair on the auditorium stage, watching Lou walk toward the podium. My feet were crossed and tucked under the chair because with Colette's sandals on, my red toenails were making me even more nervous. I kept my hands in my lap and, because I had no typed speech to clutch, I just held onto my friendship ring.

Lou set down his crisp pages, tapped the microphone, and started speaking.

"Ladies and gentlemen, boys and girls, teachers, Mrs. Johnson, my worthy opponent, Zoe Grandon, and my fellow seventh graders — good afternoon."

His voice was hitting notes as randomly as my clarinet had, the poor guy. He cleared his throat and kept going, though from my spot up there on the stage I could see that one of his knees wouldn't stay straight, so while he was delivering his typed, well-thought-out speech, he was doing a syncopated little dance with the podium. It made me root for him.

" . . . which brings me to my third proposal, which is a fund-raising project I think could benefit everybody. If we can each go to at least five businesses or relatives and convince them each to donate something worth at least ten dollars . . . "

I heard a couple of people groan in the audience and some shuffling around. Lou heard, too, and looked up, which made him lose his place on his paper. "My third proposal . . . um, hold on. OK." He smiled but didn't dare move his focus from his paper again.

As he went on, I looked out at the audience. Gabriela was watching me, and she gave me a quick thumbs-up. I had ridden over to her mom's house yesterday, and she and I made ten little posters on construction paper. She drew a pencil diagonally across each page, and along each I wrote ZOE 4 PREZ. This morning we hung them up together, and CJ helped us hand out the actual pencils to anyone who'd take one, which was pretty much everyone except Tommy and Morgan. Even Lou took one. People seemed to think the pencils were a good idea, or at least fun. I noticed a few kids writing with them on the math quiz.

Lou was on the fifth of his six proposals. I had no proposals, no ideas, no typed speech. I pictured myself doing my whacked-out clarinet scales, unprepared and failing humiliatingly. I closed my eyes.

I opened them again when the applause started. I clapped, too. Lou came and sat down on the chair next to me. "You were great," I whispered to him.

He cracked his knuckles and wished me luck.

"I'll need it," I whispered back.

"Next," said Mrs. Johnson. "Please give your attention to Zoe Grandon."

I walked up to the podium using my own normal clompy walk. I just didn't want to risk wiping out up there on the stage, especially since I'm not entirely used to Colette's sandals.

"Hi, everybody," I started. I looked out at all the people in the seats. Some of them were slumped down with their knees propped on the seat in front, some were tilted sideways, their arms propped on the armrests and their heads lolling on their fists. Some were doodling on their sneakers, some were sneaking food from lunch bags, and a few were watching me. I smiled at them.

"I'm standing up here looking out at you, thinking

what in the world can I tell these people? I tried to think of a speech all weekend. I tried to think, what can I promise? And the only thing I could come up with is a promise to do whatever you want me to do. But I can't promise that."

I took a sip from the cup of water next to me. "Oops," I said. "That's not mine. Thank you, who-ever's water I just drank."

A few people laughed.

I took a breath and said, "I can't promise to do whatever you want because, well, I'm not that good at it. I really do like to make everybody happy, even if some people don't think that's a very impressive am-bition."

I purposely avoided looking at Tommy.

"But the thing is," I said, "I guess I'm not great at guessing what everybody wants, or at being able to please everybody. And trust me, I've been trying. I've been turning myself inside out, trying to be likable, these past two weeks, but I think I've ended up annoy-ing just about everybody. Including myself. And also hurting some people who I really . . . who really mat-ter to me."

I watched Morgan's face as I said that part. Her bangs were hanging in her eyes, and her lips were in a tight, straight line. She didn't move. She didn't have her friendship ring on today again; I had looked as soon as I stepped off the bus in the morning. I don't know if we'll ever forgive each other, but we walked together from math to our lockers and from our lockers to lunch, where we sat at the same table and didn't really speak to each other. I don't know if our little clique is already wrecked or not, although Morgan was sitting between Olivia and CJ, and the seat next to CJ was empty. My seat.

I took another sip from the cup of water and wiped my mouth dry. "So — here's my big announcement — I'm done trying to be likable. If you want to vote for me, that would be great. If you don't? You know what, Lou Hochstetter is a great guy and I wouldn't blame you. I might vote for him myself. I'm sure he'd be a great president."

A few people clapped. "It's true, he would," I said, and took a deep breath before adding, "But so would I."

I leaned in to the microphone. "The thing is, there is honestly not a single person in this whole grade I don't like," I told them. I looked at CJ. "Some more than others, maybe, but still. That's the absolute truth. So I'd be, you know, happy, proud, to represent you, if you want to elect me. So if you decide you want me to be president, I promise . . ."

I tried to think of something. CJ slowly lifted one of the pencils we had made into the air. I looked at the friendship ring on her finger as she waved her wrist slightly to move the pencil around in a little rally circle.

"I promise I'll try not to annoy you," I finally said. "And I'll try to come up with some fun ideas for fundraisers and activities, and also, I promise I'll try to do my best to just . . . well, I promise I'll try to be a good friend to each of you. Thank you."

twenty-three

My red shoelace snagged on the fence as I climbed over. I unhooked it without losing my balance and managed to land on my feet in the Levits' backyard. I leaned against the fence for a few seconds to pull myself together, then stood up straight and walked slowly across their grass to the tree fort. In case anybody was watching, I wanted to be a little bit graceful.

I had to bend over double to get in there. I sat down in the back corner and looked at the palms of my hands, crusted with dirt from soccer practice. I picked a wad of grass out of my friendship ring, then spat on it to shine it up a bit. Such a pretty ring, strong and simple.

I heard a screen door slam and looked up. Tommy was walking across the lawn toward me, squinting.

When he got to the doorway of the tree fort, he rested his forearms on the roof and leaned in, below them. "You're trespassing."

I nodded. "Call the cops."

"They're on their way." I could tell he was trying not to smile, the way the corner of his mouth pulled back a little and showed his dimple. He slunk in through the doorway and sat down opposite me, against the doorjamb. At least it was the side closer to me.

"Hi," I said.

"Congratulations."

"Thanks. Did you vote for me?"

"No comment," he said. "Did you vote for yourself?"

"No comment," I said.

"Lou was a good sport."

"He's great," I said. "Shook my hand and everything, so formal."

"He took it seriously," Tommy said. He reached over and picked up a pebble that was right in front of my sneaker.

"So did I," I said.

He shrugged and tossed the pebble back and forth between his hands.

"Can we just go back to normal?" I asked.

"No."

I turned so my back was flat on the back wall of the tree fort and my legs stretched along the side wall, to right near him. I tapped him with the toe of my left sneaker and asked, "Are you gonna hate me forever?"

"No," he mumbled.

"Good." I rested my head against the side wall, watching him play with that pebble.

"Maybe another week or so, max," he said.

"Let me know when you're done."

"OK." He put the pebble down in the doorway.

"I'd trade winning this election if I could, to make you stop hating me."

"No you wouldn't," he said.

"I might."

"Don't say that," he whispered. "Just . . ." He reached over and stuck his finger through the loop of my shoelace, then twisted his finger so my shoelace was wound tight around it.

We stayed like that for a little while.

Rachel Vail has written four other well-received novels for adolescents, including WONDER, an *American Bookseller* "Pick of the Lists"; DARING TO BE ABIGAIL, a *School Library Journal* Best Book of the Year; DO-OVER, a Recommended Book for Reluctant Young Readers; and EVER AFTER, which was one of the New York Public Library's 100 Best Children's Books in 1994. The Friendship Ring series has received strong praise from reviewers and was listed as one of *Publishers Weekly*'s Best Books of 1998.

Rachel Vail lives with her husband and two sons in New York City.

Have you met all the girls in The Friendship Ring?

Zoe. C.J. Morgan. Olivia.

The Friendship Ring Series

 By Rachel Vail

$3.99 each!

☐ BDM 0-439-08761-9 **#1: If You Only Knew**

☐ BDM 0-439-08762-7 **#2: Please, Please, Please**

☐ BDM 0-439-08763-5 **#3: Not That I Care**

☐ BDM 0-590-37454-0 **#4: What Are Friends For?**

☐ BDM 0-590-68911-8 **#5: Popularity Contest**